# FACELIFT

# TRACE SHERER
# LIZA ANDREWS

# FACELIFT

A NOVEL

ARE YOU DYING TO LOOK GOOD?

*To Trevor and Preston.*

*—Trace*

*To Candi, whose love is a magical scalpel, healing the deepest wounds and making the entire universe prettier.*

*—Liza*

# ACKNOWLEDGMENTS

*A special thank you to Juana, who found a printed copy of the novel that I wrote twenty-five years ago in a random battery drawer in my current home, and to Liza, who turned that novel into something special. Candi, my co-dreamer and editor. Thank you, Kimi, Michael, Mush, Fran, Richard, Jim, Scott, and every other person who has dreamed out loud with me and helped me to achieve those dreams and so much more.*

*—Trace J. Sherer*

*My deepest gratitude to my dear friend and co-author Trace Sherer for this collaboration, our mega-talented editor, Candi Cross, for her indispensable trained eye and precious advice, and our marvelous copyeditor, Caroline Clouse. A heartfelt thank you to Cristhiane Vieira for her enormous support of my literary efforts along the years, and my dream creative team, Angela, Wilton, Sandra, and Gisele, for their critique, suggestions, and research. I interviewed numerous patients of plastic surgery before and while preparing this manuscript, and I thank them now in anonymity, which is how they would prefer it, for sharing their experiences, fears, expectations, and medical mistakes involved in their aesthetic procedures. I'd like to thank Dr. Mohamed Soliman for his insights on hospital culture. Dr. Dione Ammon, who answered all my questions on plastic surgery and showed me the importance of having realistic expectations to avoid identity problems. And finally, Dr. Ivo Pitanguy, deceased in 2016, whom I met in my twenties and respectfully used as a character in this novel in an effort to keep his memory alive and pay homage to his brilliant work. A genius plastic surgeon, globally known as the Michelangelo of the scalpel, Pitanguy operated on celebrities and royalty from all over the world with the same enthusiasm he taught his students and did pro bono work for those with limited means. He believed that, rich or poor, everyone deserved to live well with their self-esteem. May his incredible skills and altruistic ideals live on in his apprentices worldwide.*

*—Liza Andrews*

# BOSTON

———

## JANUARY 1986

# 1

RICHARD WILKEN AWOKE from the nap that followed his fabulous orgasm. *This kind of sex should be illegal.* Not because he was engaged to someone else or because the attractive brunette beside him was married to another man. Their chemistry was so rare it felt deliciously wrong and almost unfair to the rest of humanity. Besides, fucking a man's wife in his own bed was a power game that gave Richard the ultimate high.

He could picture Dr. John Landry, stiff as the corpses under his scalpel, working night shifts. Would Landry's blood warm up a bit if he caught his wife cheating? The risk increased Richard's excitement, and to make his life easier, the Landrys' street had no security cameras, and he and Sally Landry could sneak in and out as they pleased.

Still laughing, Richard turned to Sally and whispered, "Wake up, pretty. I'll heat up that pizza." Top of their class since Harvard Medical School, he and Sally were currently finishing their specialization in plastic surgery. Equally adventurous, with the same love for mixing booze, cocaine, and rough sex, they tried to match their schedules to be together twice a month.

Their escapades were becoming as dangerous as they were thrilling. That evening, as in their previous three dates, they had been drinking, snorting, and having sex in the Landrys' home.

"Come on," Richard said in regular volume. Sally was a heavy sleeper, particularly when she was drunk. "We need to change these linens."

He reached out to shake his lover, and her irresponsive body made him jump.

The room was only partially illuminated by the bathroom lights, and Richard turned on the bedside lamp and checked for Sally's pulse. Nothing. He first assumed it was an overdose, then saw the purple marks on her neck and realized their usual strangling game had gone too far, too close to his climax. As they were both deeply intoxicated, Sally did not protest, and he'd squeezed harder than intended. It wasn't the first time they had fallen into deep sleep right after their sexual marathons, and he didn't notice anything strange.

*Shit!* Richard liked Sally. A shame she was now trying to ruin his life.

John Landry had in his job a perfect alibi, and the police would know someone else had been with his wife. Richard's medical mind began to picture an autopsy.

They would find cocaine, whisky, and *his* semen. Sally took the pill, and he never wore a condom. That once convenient detail could put him behind bars. Richard was also aware of how discreet they had been and that a semen match would only be required if he became a suspect.

Trained to think quickly, Richard made a choice. Even if he could prove it had been an accident, that would be an irreparable stain on his reputation. All would have been in vain. His efforts to go to Harvard, to be number one in his program, and mostly, to gain the heart of a millionaire's daughter about to open the doors to his wildest dreams.

He was only thirty-three, awfully young to become a martyr. Sally's death had to be the product of a robbery gone wrong.

Richard found a pair of rubber gloves under the kitchen sink, some paper towels, and bleach. He cleaned every surface, including the knobs of every door he had passed through. Even if he couldn't recall his steps to that bed, he focused on eliminating any traces of the unfortunate journey.

He kept moving fast. Deliberately, he broke two reading lamps in the living room. Three cactus pots landed on the floor, spreading earth on the rug and creating an immediate sense of chaos. Back in the bedroom, Richard opened drawers and spread their contents around the bed and vanity table. He took a few paintings off the walls, simulating a thief seeking valuables. The Landrys owned no safe; that was just to look professional. Sally's watch, wedding ring, and wallet would go with him. They would sink easily in the Charles River and there would be evidence that something had actually been taken. The final touch to avoid suspicion that Sally had allowed the murderer in was to find a tool kit and break the door lock.

Another twenty minutes would elapse before Richard was done with the place and ready for the hardest part of his coverup. Having seen enough victims of rape, he knew exactly how Sally's body should look like.

# 2

THE STREETS WERE wet following the first snow of the year, and the January wind threatened to freeze Richard Wilken's face as he hurried to Beth Israel Hospital that morning. On days like this, daydreams of becoming a famous plastic surgeon often warmed him more than his Burberry coat, the lapels of which were up to his ears.

At nine years old, Richard already knew he would become a doctor like his father and grandfather. Both cardiologists had introduced the human body to Richard as a fabulous machine whose engines were cared for by the smartest, most devoted men. Whenever possible, Richard's father took him to home visits. Most patients were regular people whose lifestyles resembled their own. Families who lived in the suburbs of Westchester or in small apartments in Manhattan. That was Richard's middle-class world and he barely noticed there was anything beyond it. They lived in Dobbs Ferry, and that Saturday morning Richard's father took him to the city. The plan was to go to the Metropolitan Museum of Art after his father checked on a patient recovering from a heart attack.

Mr. Bloom lived on Fifth Avenue across the street from Central Park. As they stepped into the lobby, Richard found a wonderland of gloved doormen, concierges, crystal chandeliers, and enormous flower arrangements. A golden elevator led them straight to Mr. Bloom's door and Richard whispered, "Does he own the entire floor, Dad?"

"That's correct."

A uniformed maid opened the door, and the apartment was like Richard's beloved museums. Head turning in all directions, he took in the high ceilings with elaborate molding, the paintings, the sculptures. How could his father's patient afford such fabulous things?

Finally, Richard caught sight of an old man sitting by the window and started to follow his father, his eyes never leaving the breathtaking views of the park.

"Wait here," his father said halfway through. "I won't take long."

"I wanna talk to him."

"No, son. This patient needs privacy."

"Bring the boy over, Dr. Wilken," said the hoarse voice across the long wooded-paneled room. "I love kids."

Richard smiled and rushed forward. He was shy

with no one. "Thank you for allowing me to observe, sir! I'm Richard Wilken and I wanna be a doctor."

The old man found that very amusing. "Good for you!"

"May I ask what you do? You seem to make a lot of money."

"Richard!" His father's face was flushed with embarrassment. "That was rude. Apologize to Mr. Bloom."

"Sorry."

Mr. Bloom did not mind at all. The boy's ambition was fascinating. "That's all right. A young man needs to plan his career." Mr. Bloom's laughter was genuine, contained by something sore inside his chest. "I was an investment banker. A nerve-racking job that's highly responsible for my heart condition. This is my son's home. He's a plastic surgeon and makes money all right."

That day, Richard realized his father and grandfather were doing something wrong. Twenty years later, he knew exactly what. They had been the nice doctors who did pro bono work and accepted every shitty insurance plan. They knew nothing of luxury and barely paid their mortgages before dying.

*One doesn't need over a decade of studies to do charity.* Richard had worked hard, and if he played his cards well today, wealth and power would be finally within his grasp. He just needed to survive this Sally Landry issue.

By now, Sally's husband must have found her. The news would hit the hospital any minute if it hadn't already, and the police might show up to ask questions. The hospital façade came to sight and, unlike most men in his position, Richard calmly walked those final steps to the revolving doors going through his mental script. It wouldn't be his first time lying about serious matters or being interrogated by the cops.

He found five of his colleagues in the locker room. Two males and three females from different specialties. While Richard recognized all the faces, the only name that mattered to him was the black man's, Phillips, a genius in neuro. He always addressed the rest as "doctors" without their last names.

The group's distressed-looking conversation and the whispered words *crime* and *robbery* hinted they already knew about Sally. "Good morning, doctors!" Richard said as he headed to his locker.

"Have you heard about Sally?" asked the male resident beside Phillips. He was specializing in anesthesiology. Not particularly memorable, the man constantly found excuses to approach Richard.

Richard offered an expression of concern. "No. Is she all right?"

"She was murdered."

"God, what happened?"

"We're not sure. The rumor's just started to spread."

Richard shook his head and, facing his locker, began replacing his regular coat with a white one. "I can't believe it. Sally and I were taking last night off, and I joked that she should sleep for twelve hours like I would."

He turned back to study his colleagues' expressions. His comment landed with no suspicion, and if needed, he could repeat it to the police.

"Apparently Sally took your advice and stayed home," said a female resident from cardio. "I heard someone broke in and she was badly beaten. Maybe raped."

"Let's not get ahead of ourselves," Phillips said. "The hospital's making a formal statement soon."

Dr. Barclay was the attending physician for the plastic surgery program. An extremely skinny man with hollow eyes and very accentuated cheek bones, he supervised Richard and Sally in their patients' care, and behind his back, residents called him "Skull." It'd been a joke since their introductory class, where the man stood beside a real skeleton on display. It took enormous effort from the residents not to laugh at the resemblance between the two.

Barclay looked even bonier that morning standing in the residents' lounge to deliver the news of Sally Landry's murder. "This hospital's administration can't describe the sadness we all feel for Dr. Landry's unacceptable fate." He talked about Sally's flawless character, her great accomplishments since medical school, and how much patients and hospital staff liked her.

Listening to Barclay, Richard almost believed Sally was that saint. The two of them were also alike when it came to their professional ambitions. He could still

11

hear Sally say, "It's exhausting playing the nice doc! Thank goodness I'm a great actress." She laughed and licked Richard's chin. "If I can fake orgasms to keep a happy hubby, I can fake anything for my dream job."

As they made their rounds during that final year, Richard and Sally discovered the types of fools who would become their ideal patients: wealthy men and women with terrible self-esteem.

One day, before checking a woman's nose job, done for the third time simply to achieve perfection, and another's facelift, trying to trick nature in twenty years, Sally whispered to Richard, "Look at these two. We can make millions and never have a patient again!"

He fought a smile. "In theory, they are patients, Dr. Landry."

Sally's eyes told him, *You know what I mean*, and she entered the room beaming at the women she had just mocked.

Richard did know what Sally meant and he agreed. With the exceptions of those with deformities or victims of accidents, patients doing plastic surgery should not even be called *patients* or their doctors. Those were cosmetic procedures. As Sally defined them, "haircuts performed with a scalpel."

Richard would miss Sally. In an alternate universe where they didn't need money to achieve their goals, they could have been a perfect couple. Sally had made only one mistake Richard wouldn't: marrying out of love. His mother had left when he was little, and Sally herself was banging another man under her husband's roof. Richard knew how love ended.

Dr. Barclay was now talking about the murder, and Richard tuned in to find out how the police had read his staged crime scene.

"Someone broke into Dr. Landry's home while her husband was at work."

*Check.*

"The intruder was looking for valuables and took all he could find."

*Check.*

"The police still don't know whether Dr. Landry was home when they broke in or walked into the scene and was attacked by the intruder."

*Check.*

Richard started to relax. Next should be talking about the rape. There would be gasping and murmuring, and some women always started to cry. Everything was so straightforward that maybe the police wouldn't even show up at the hospital.

Then Dr. Barclay added, "Dr. Landry's husband would have only found her this morning when he returned from work, but he got an anonymous call urging him to rush home last night. He arrived shortly after nine thirty, and it was already too late."

*What?* Richard had left Sally's place at nine fifteen after ensuring there wasn't a soul around. Who would have placed that call, and what would they have heard or seen?

"Lamentably," Dr. Barclay proceeded, "This possible witness still didn't show up. The police are investigating the case and may wish to talk to some of you. Be ready to cooperate."

The meeting was over and despite the buzz of lingering conversation, the residents dissipated to begin their rounds. Richard remained frozen until the guy in anesthesia who had delivered the news materialized beside him again. "Piece of shit, huh? What do you think happened?"

Richard wished Dr. Nobody would leave him alone. "Hard to say. I'm so shocked."

They merged into the small crowd waiting for the elevators, with Dr. Nobody blabbing. Richard registered his final sentences. "Sally was great. Will definitely be missed."

The two men stepped into the elevator and on the second floor went separate ways.

Richard's first patient was a burn victim from a car crash. The man had had multiple surgeries, was on heavy painkillers, was always irritated, and asked too many questions. Richard headed to the men's room to calm his nerves first. He locked himself in a stall and sat on the toilet. The police would come, he had no doubt, and he needed a tighter script than the one he had initially prepared. What if someone had seen him? How on earth could any excuse be remotely believable?"

*You got this.* In medical school, Richard had discovered a nerve-taming technique to block his emotions. It consisted of controlling his heart rate as he lied to people. He had applied it to anyone from hospital staff and colleagues to friends and lovers until he mastered it. After a while, truth and lies felt the same to him, and even though he had never tried, Richard was confident he could trick a polygraph.

He took a deep breath and focused on the small engine beating inside his chest. Another deep breath and a black screen appeared on his mind. He kept breathing in and out and his heart started to slow down. His mind found a door on the black screen and he walked through it.

He was twenty-three years old.

Medical school.

Theresa Dawson's alleged suicide.

The detective interrogating him.

Richard relived scene after scene, line after line, as if they were part of a movie in which he was acting. He did it twice. After a moment in silence, he opened his eyes with the serenity of a man who could foresee his future.

Someone was standing by the sink, and Richard flushed the toilet. He and the stranger exchanged nods, and Richard washed his hands and headed out to start his day.

By lunchtime, the police were already interviewing residents and hospital staff. Around three o'clock, Richard was paged and went to the designated conference room where a female detective sat at the head of the table.

She was around forty years old, her brown hair

pulled back, taking any softness out of her face. She wore a gray suit and black shoes that made her look masculine. Perhaps intentionally. "Good afternoon," she said, indicating where she wanted Richard to sit down. "Dr. Richard Wilken, right?"

"Yes. How can I help you?"

"I'm Detective Berman. I'm investigating the murder of your colleague, Sally Landry. I'm sure you've heard."

"Yes. Still hasn't sunk in."

"You're in her program. How well did you know her?"

Richard's greatest lesson from when Theresa Dawson died was that being evasive or playing dumb during an investigation just made detectives more suspicious. "I knew Sally pretty well," he said. "We often discussed our patients' issues, and I highly valued her opinion. She was a wonderful colleague and very bright."

Detective Berman looked down to take notes. Eyes on Richard again, she asked, "Did you talk about personal subjects as well?"

"Sometimes. I'm engaged and Sally was married, so I remember once she warned me about the challenges of starting a family being a doctor."

"Will you miss her?"

"A lot." Richard's eyes never wandered, and his facial expression reflected honest pain. "Sally was one of my favorite colleagues. Had we had more time, we could have become close friends."

Detective Berman took more notes and casually asked, "Were you attracted to her?"

Ricard knew that was coming. It always did. "Sally was an attractive lady, detective. I think most men in this hospital found her attractive."

"Would that include yourself?"

"Yes. But we never flirted. I'm in love with my fiancée."

"And did Dr. Landry seem happily married?"

"She never told me otherwise."

"Dr. Wilken, she had a considerable amount of alcohol and cocaine in her blood. Do you know if she had a drug habit?"

"I don't believe she did. Sally wouldn't see patients until this morning. If she was drinking or taking recreational drugs last night, I guess she was just trying to relax."

"Do you also do cocaine, Dr. Wilken?"

"On rare occasions."

"Do you know whom Dr. Landry used to socialize with?"

"I can't say I do."

Detective Berman slid a sheet of paper across the table. "According to this list provided by the hospital, you were off last night as well. Do you mind telling me what you did?"

"Not at all. I was planning to see my fiancée, but she was busy with her functions at the Harvard Art Museums, so I took the evening to catch up on my sleep."

"Thank you for your cooperation. Here's my card. Please call me if you think of anything else."

"Of course, Detective."

When Richard was halfway to the door, Detective Berman said, "One more question."

"Yes."

"Have you ever been to Dr. Landry's home?"

Richard hoped the police wouldn't ask that question. Either Detective Berman was fishing, or she already knew the answer.

"I never had the pleasure. Sally suggested having dinner when both our partners were available. But her husband worked night shifts and it never happened."

Richard waited, aware that if someone had seen him, he would leave the building in handcuffs.

Detective Berman seemed satisfied and concluded the interrogation.

At seven p.m., Richard and several of his colleagues watched the local news about the murder. Two reporters took turns relaying the case. "It seems a robbery followed by a fatal attack claimed the life of Dr. Sally Landry in East Boston last night. A mysterious individual warned her husband about an emergency while he was at work. The individual remains unknown."

The other reporter jumped in. "The call came from a pay phone close to the Landrys' home. What doesn't make sense is why the caller didn't dial 911. And if they knew the victim's husband well enough to call him, why not reveal their name?"

A devastated John Landry appeared on the screen. "I didn't care who called me. My wife wasn't picking up the phone and I rushed home."

The reporter continued, "The hospital operator who received the anonymous message on Dr. John Landry's behalf said the caller seemed to be a man, but the voice wasn't deep enough for her to be sure. The police will continue to investigate, and we'll bring you updates."

Still staring at the TV, Richard replayed the scene of his leaving Sally's house through the back door after shutting off all the lights in the yard. There wasn't a soul on the street, and the neighboring houses on both sides and across from Sally's were too distant for someone to make out a face in the dark, so who was this caller?

Richard's thoughts were interrupted by his colleagues' various speculations.

"The reporter's right. Why would someone doing a good deed remain anonymous?"

Another resident shouted. "It was probably one of the gang members trying to screw his partners."

"I hate to say it," said a third resident, "but they won't find this guy. If the caller was able to identify the murderer, by now a police sketch would be circulating."

Richard found some solace in this final observation and left the TV lounge. His body and mind were craving the twelve-hour sleep he told everyone he had enjoyed the night before. After the past surreal twenty-four hours, Richard had no desire to see his fiancée. Unfortunately, that was nonnegotiable. He had spent two years cultivating that cash cow and couldn't risk losing the marriage so near the finish line. Most importantly, in case of a deeper investigation, he needed to get his story straight so Constance wouldn't accidentally contradict what he'd told the police.

After his long shift, Richard changed and left the hospital. In the cab heading to Constance's home, he recalled how he had met her.

# BOSTON

———

## TWO YEARS EARLIER

# 3

CHRISTOPHER PARSON, ONE of Richard's wealthy colleagues, was attending a fundraising event at Harvard Art Museums that week.

"I hate this stuff, but my mom's in the committee and she insists that I attend this one." Parson's face was amusingly desperate, as if the young resident was about to endure brain surgery himself. "Other than us, victimized offspring of the organizers, it'll be a bunch of dinosaurs. Please join me, Wilken, so this will be less unbearable."

Richard chuckled. Rich people could be so dramatic. "Count me in. We'll make it fun."

"That's my man!" Parson said with clear relief; then he seemed to remember that Richard wasn't a millionaire. "Got a tux? If not, I'll be glad to—"

"No worries. I do."

Richard's love for wealth had begun in that marvelous Fifth Avenue apartment when he was a boy and had only grown stronger along the years. Even though he couldn't magically become rich, he quickly understood the power of appearance to opening doors.

As a teenager, Richard's hobby was heading to Manhattan to do two things: flirt with the glamorous plastic surgery offices on the Upper East Side and window shop on Madison Avenue. He watched the fancy stores from the outside after discovering that he was not welcomed by the salespeople even when wearing his Sunday's best. He absorbed the styles and textures of each outfit on the mannequins and observed the elegant clients who frequented those places. Richard started to imitate the way rich people walked and talked and realized that if he mastered the art of conversation and looked the part, the sophisticated crowd would feel comfortable hanging out with him.

After covering Madison Avenue from 80th Street to 53rd, he headed to Lexington Avenue and spent hours browsing Bloomingdale's. In department stores, Richard could touch those precious garments and even try them on. He loved the way they felt. Cashmere smelled like a happy Christmas. One that in Richard's imagination was still to come.

At fifteen, he saved several months of his allowance and bought himself an Hermès scarf. That gave him the satisfaction of buying his first designer piece and the opportunity to become friendly with a young salesman who filled the gaps in his observations.

"Think of brands as a way to distinguish social tribes, Richard. When you first meet someone, you don't know who they are, so you need visual signs to help you categorize them."

"By their clothes?"

"Exactly. Clothes, jewelry, and accessories are the fastest way to find out who is loaded and who isn't."

Richard went through the men's catalogue shaking his head. "I understand quality, but why does a designer's suit cost so much more than a regular one in the same fabric?"

"Well, fashion designers took the word *elite* to a whole new level. By charging more for something that seems the same, they create a clientele who pays more to be exclusive. It's like a membership. All clubs have a pool, but some are popular; others are for the blue bloods."

After Richard learned enough about what to wear, he expanded his curiosity to other departments. Head high, wearing his new scarf, he entered the jewelry department of Bergdorf Goodman like he belonged. Hands behind his back, he went through the different displays like a connoisseur. When he found the largest gems, he smiled and told the saleswoman, "My father is a busy doctor. He asked me to look for a nice ring for my mother's birthday. What would you recommend?"

That went well, and Richard's next stop was Tiffany's.

While Richard's mother might have left him, for years she helped him immerse himself in the world of the rich. A smart teenager trying to buy a chic present for his mother turned out to be the perfect act to hook salespeople. Even in the fanciest stores. Both men and women didn't care if Richard would actually be able to afford the expensive gifts he inquired about. They appreciated his intentions and fed him all the information he wanted, from French perfumes to Persian rugs and Baccarat crystals. The more familiar Richard became with those magnificent items, the more he knew he would do anything so that one day he could be surrounded by them.

As a grown man, Richard still couldn't afford everything he needed, so he started investing in key pieces for his wardrobe during his residency years. Even though the crazy hours in the hospital and the sleep deprivation didn't allow him to go out much, he knew that when the days to meet the right people came, he should be ready. Richard's first acquisition was a high-quality classic suit, then two designer ties, a pair of Italian shoes, and gradually he populated his wardrobe with the fundamental pieces he needed for the character he wanted to play.

The tuxedo had been a recent acquisition and Richard was wearing it for the first time. The first of many, he thought, looking at himself in the mirror. He looked sharp. Taller than his six feet. Richard's father had given him a Cartier watch when he graduated from medical school and left him a pair of Tiffany cufflinks as an heirloom. He was wearing both that evening.

Two years of specialty in plastics surgery still

awaited Richard at Harvard. Afterward, he was considering trying his luck back in New York or heading to Miami, where he had some good colleagues. Boston was not Richard's first option, and yet, he networked at every chance. If working there ended up being the case, tonight's party, tickets for which cost a grand per head, would be a great opportunity to make fruitful connections.

Richard met Parson's parents, who, too busy entertaining friends, said quick hellos as they shook hands but did not engage in conversation. Richard "went to the men's room," his usual excuse to walk around by himself, and studied the crowd. Most of the attendees were in their fifties or older, the women wearing flashy jewelry. Real ones, with big diamonds. A middle-aged redhead caught Richard staring and held his gaze. She misread his eyes on her Chopard emeralds and, believing he was looking at her cleavage, smiled. Richard smiled back and returned to his table.

Parson's sister had arrived with a friend, and they were sitting with him. Parson looked up and said, "Ladies, this is my genius friend Richard Wilken. Richard, my sister, Milla, and this is Constance Carlton. They graduated in fine art last year."

Milla seemed even shorter and skinnier beside her curvaceous friend. Richard shook Milla's hand first with a "Nice to meet you," then focused on Constance.

She was five foot eight with timid green eyes and shoulder-length blond hair.

"Constance's father is the real estate king in Houston," Parson added, as if tipping his middle-class friend. "Constance works at the museum and helped organize this beautiful event."

Richard offered his best smile and shook Constance's hand. "Nice to meet you, and thank you for this. It's a lovely party."

"Thank you."

Richard was never the most handsome man in the room. His features were as plain as the guy next door, and yet, the confident way he carried himself was extremely attractive to women. By the way Constance lingered holding his hand, he knew she liked him.

There were no free seats beside Constance, so Richard stood. "What kind of work do you do here?"

Before Constance could reply, Milla got up. "Sit here, Richard. I'll catch up with my brother."

Richard and Constance chatted about their current work, their experiences studying at Harvard, and what they enjoyed doing in Boston. At some point, Constance said, "I had to do something related to the arts. Both my parents' families have been in real estate or construction for generations. I can't stand either of these topics."

"Noted!"

"And which are your forbidden topics, Dr. Wilken?"

"Sports. I never cared for them."

"I thought sports were ingrained in the male brain!"

Richard's laughter felt like chocolate fudge to Constance. Even though she didn't consider herself funny, she did her best to keep that pleasant sound coming.

In Richard's opinion, Constance was smart and not bad looking; she simply lacked the sex appeal of confident people. Apparently, there was something amiss that money could not buy. He intended to find out what. They danced, and at the end of the evening, Richard said, "I'd love to continue our conversation. Would you join me for dinner on Wednesday?"

Richard and Constance had dinner that week and the next. On the third, they watched a movie after dining at a charming French bistro, and the evening, as always, ended with Richard's putting Constance in a cab.

Living near the hospital was a small luxury Richard allowed himself after his father passed away and left him a house in the suburbs. He sold the house and invested the money so he could move to an elegant one-bedroom in the heart of the city. The rent was twice what he could afford before getting a well-paying job. Still, he did the math and decided it was worth the investment. In that building, he met well-to-do fellows like Parson and a member of the country club who initiated him in golf.

Constance lived in a townhouse in Beacon Hill, one of the most expensive parts of Boston, and had a chef and a personal assistant. The more Richard learned about Constance's sophisticated lifestyle and her family's power in Houston, the more into her he was.

The way Constance looked at Richard every time they met was a clear sign that she was romantically interested. Though for some reason she had never invited him to her place. Not even given him a kiss. Things needed to move faster.

On their fourth date, Richard chose a restaurant near his place, and when they walked by his building after dinner, he said, "This is home. Would you like to come up for a glass of wine?"

Constance stared up at the building as if deliberating. She had doubled her anxiety meds to avoid thinking of that moment. It'd been ages since she'd enjoyed a man's company. She was attracted to everything about Richard, from his wit to his biceps, and she'd wanted to sleep with him since the night they met.

"Constance?"

"Sorry, I was appreciating the façade."

"Do you wanna come up?"

*Yes,* she thought. Sex, however, was for the one-nighters she met in nightclubs and never saw again. Not for perfect men like Richard. There was no way she would disappoint him in bed. No way she would survive his rejection. "I guess next time," she said.

Richard produced a sad sigh almost as authentic as his real frustration. "I don't think you like me the way I like you. You want us to be friends, right?"

Constance forced a smile. "Of course, you must be a disaster in the sack."

Richard laughed. "You think so?"

"I'm positive. Harvard doctors know nothing of women's anatomy."

"I'm sorry if any of my colleagues have disappointed. Would you allow me to clear our reputation?"

While Constance was pleased that her jokes had lightened the mood, Richard's face was too close for her to remain in character. She kissed his cheek and said, "You're amazing. I just don't sleep around."

"I don't want only sex. I want to date you."

Constance stared at him. Richard could pass as wealthy, but from their multiple conversations, she knew he was middle-class, which inevitably raised a red flag. She wished there was a magical way to reveal if he liked her as he would like a woman from his world. Mostly, Constance wished Richard could like her enough to overlook her terrible flaw.

None of these wishes were possible. Her father was right—whoever dated or even married her would do it for the cash. Her flaw was far too big for any men to overlook.

Constance's eyes filled with tears and Richard wondered if she had suffered some kind of abuse. Psychology would be crucial here. He gently held her hands. "I care about you, Constance, and the last thing I want is to make you cry."

"It's nothing you've done."

"Do you wanna talk about it? I can make you a cup of tea, or we can walk around the block and—"

Constance wrapped her arms around Richard's neck and kissed him. For a moment, she didn't care what would happen next. She wanted to feel normal, pretend Richard loved her.

Constance's kiss was desperate, a hungry animal feeding from his mouth. Now Richard had no doubts something was very wrong with that woman. He hoped he could use it in his favor. When Constance detached from his lips, he tried to look radiant. "Come, darling."

Hand in hand, Richard guided Constance through the lobby, and her heart was drumming somewhere outside her body. She could hear it louder with every step.

As if fearing Constance's hesitation might return, Richard kissed her in the elevator all the way to the seventh floor. Mercifully, his apartment was the first unit to the right, and with a quick turn of his key, they were inside.

Another long kiss and this time Richard's hands traveled from Constance's face to her neck and down her spine, appraising her back, her butt, and coming up again.

She stopped him. "Where's the bedroom?"

Richard smiled. "That way, ma'am."

"Wait for me there."

Constance went to the bathroom and in autopilot repeated the production she offered her one-nighters. When she entered the bedroom, Richard was leaning against the headboard in his boxers. "Hot body," Constance said, and desire made her forget her discomfort.

"You look gorgeous," Richard said, and he meant it. Constance looked more like an escort than a high-society woman. Her hair was up, and she had retouched her mascara and put on a darker lipstick. She wore her long-sleeved black top and high heels. Her skirt and panties were gone.

Richard had decided to let Constance take the lead.

He waited, and after a moment she walked toward him. She stood and without a hint of romance said, "I won't blow you. I don't do anal or anything violent. And you won't try to remove my shoes or my top. I will leave if you touch these parts of my body. Still interested?"

"Very."

"Get naked."

# 4

RICHARD REMOVED HIS boxers and slid down the mattress. Lying on his back, he remained immobile, only his head following Constance's movements.

She crawled into the bed and slowly caressed his body from chest to pelvis, like she was claiming him. Without a word, she sat on his erection and started to ride him.

Richard reached out for Constance's face first, his right thumb circling her painted lips. Obedient, he skipped her torso and gently played with her belly button and pubic hair. She moaned. Richard grabbed her hips and increased the speed of his thrusts. Constance's eyes were closed, her face toward the ceiling. She moaned louder and Richard knew she was close. Her body was tightening around him, and his hand scooped between her legs, pushing her to her climax.

Feeling powerful, watching Constance's surrender, Richard let himself go.

Constance dismounted Richard as soon as he was done and to his surprise, instead of lying beside him, she headed to the bathroom and closed the door.

*Okay...* When he heard the shower running, he got up and knocked. "Is everything all right?"

"Yes," said the disembodied voice behind the door. "Will be right there."

Constance resurfaced fully dressed, her hair down and her makeup as inconspicuous as it had been during dinner. "I'll take it back," she said. "Harvard docs know a thing or two. I may even come back." She tried in vain to sound excessively playful. The whole scene was artificial from the beginning.

Richard had put on a robe and was sitting at the edge of the bed, serious as Constance had never seen him. "Would you please sit here with me."

"Richard it's late. I—"

"Please?"

Constance sat beside Richard. Not close enough for their shoulders to rub.

"I thought we were great together," he said, "but now I'm at a loss. Can you please tell me what's going on?"

"Nothing is going on, darling. We had a great time and now I'm leaving."

"Leaving for tonight or for good?"

Constance could take no more talking. "Richard,

you wanted to fuck me and you did. What else do you want?"

"Honesty. Respect. You're not the only one who has feelings here. Are you involved with someone else?"

"Of course not! I just don't wanna take this too seriously."

"Because doctors have crazy schedules?"

She chuckled.

"Or because I'm not rich?"

Constance averted her eyes and Richard took a deep breath. "I understand."

He stood up and took Constance's hand for her to follow him. "I'll call the doorman to get you a cab, and I'll take the friendship offer, if it's still on the table."

She looked at him. "Sorry. I don't believe that's possible."

Richard hated wasting time. Despite his act before Constance left his apartment, he didn't think money was the problem. There was something edgy and unpredictable about her. Sometimes she was emotional and easy to manipulate; other times, her decisions had a core of steel. He knew there was no way he could have done better. By the time he pushed Constance a little, she should be ready… or she would never be.

Richard had left her a voice message the following morning. "Hi, I hope you'll change your mind and call me. I miss you." He spent a week trying to decipher what had gone wrong with Constance. After ten days without news, he considered her gone and his focus shifted back to his professional projects. Short of a month later, Richard received a message asking if he'd like to dine at Constance's home. He smiled. *Of course I do.*

Constance had spent a miserable month in inner struggle. She desperately missed Richard and it had required supernatural determination not to return his call.

Instead, she had called Dr. Kessler, her psychiatrist in Houston for over a decade, every other day.

Only a week ago, Dr. Kessler had reminded her, "You have an addictive personality. No drugs, no alcohol, and no out-of-your-league men you can obsess over."

Constance's mouth would reply, "Yes, Doctor," but her mind had absorbed Richard and refused to let him go. After their fabulous sex, her cravings were both emotional and physical. While Dr. Kessler spoke, his voice gave way to more powerful sensorial memories: the scent of Richard's hair, the warmth of his skin, the taste of his mouth. Constance knew she should have never tried him.

Dr. Kessler went mute, aware that his patient was no longer with him. Constance Carlton was a hopeless case he hadn't given up on for one reason: not to enrage her prominent parents, who made generous donations to his clinic.

To Kessler, the intriguing part of Constance's obsessions with men was her definition of *out of her league.* For most, the wealthy and famous were beyond reach. Constance was royalty; and yet, to her, impossible men were the extra-confident peasants with sexy bodies and brilliant brains. It had been that way since she was sixteen.

"Are you with me, Constance?" Kessler asked after a long pause. "Can we continue?"

"Sorry, Doctor."

"What were you thinking about?"

"Steve."

And even though he expected that, Kessler suppressed a sigh. Steve had worked for the Carltons long ago; he was the gardener's son. Constance's first love and lover.

"Please walk me through it."

"You've heard it a thousand times."

"Pretend I haven't. If it's bothering you, you need to let it out."

Constance could still see the eighteen-year-old boy with his unruly brown hair and almond eyes. Despite his humble origins, Steve was ambition personified and Constance was immediately drawn to him. They secretly dated along her adolescence and to please Steve, she had attempted two surgeries to fix her problem. "Richard reminds me of Steve and I'm keeping my distance because I'm scared."

"Tell me why this relationship scares you."

Constance felt like crying recalling the surgeries, the pain. None had been successful, and the last one had made her problem worse. Steve could not love her with that deformity. Out of shame, she had swallowed a bottle of sleeping pills.

"I know this is tough," Kessler said, "but talk to me."

"I'm afraid of everything. His rejection would be crushing, and because I'm rich, his acceptance would be suspicious. I don't know what to think."

Kessler considered Constance's self-preservation logical and however haphazard, a sign of growth. She had survived her suicide attempt because she was found in time by a housemaid, and after a week in the hospital she'd been released under his psychiatric care. "Do you still remember how you felt about your father then?" Kessler asked.

"How could I forget?" When Constance returned home, Steve and his father had been dismissed. She was furious for several days. Then the anger vanished as if she'd had a revelation. That was her father's way to protect her.

"Do you still think your father is the only man capable of loving you the way you are?"

Constance hesitated. "No. My father thinks I'm a freak."

"Let's discuss what your father thinks at another session. Now focus on Richard. If you changed your mind about who makes you feel safe, you may be starting to open your heart to new possibilities."

With that in mind, Constance had no more need to call Dr. Kessler or to avoid Richard. What happened while she was in love with Steve was over a decade ago, and maybe, only maybe, she could give Richard a chance. He was a doctor, after all. If someone could understand what she'd gone through, that someone was him.

Constance looked at her watch. Richard would be arriving soon. She lit the candles and was proud of the table she had put together. She had hurt Richard, making him feel unworthy of her. Inviting him over was a way to welcome him into her world and, even if for a while, into her heart.

The phone rang, startling her. Judging by the hour, it was probably her mother. The loud ringing disturbed the atmosphere. Her family should not know that she was taking chances with a man who could benefit from her money. Her father would repeat those horrible things she did not want to hear again. No, she wouldn't answer the phone or share her little adventure with anyone yet. It would be challenging to heat up the food and serve the wine on her own, but giving her staff the evening off would provide her the privacy she needed for her experiment.

Richard brought Constance orchids and an expensive bottle of pinot noir. "Good evening, Ms. Carlton."

Constance was thrilled to see him, just hated the overwhelming effect Richard had on her. After a month apart, her hands were trembling when she collected his gifts. She wasn't ready to touch him yet. Without a hug or a kiss, she said, "Please, come on in."

41

That evening was particularly chilly. Constance waited for Richard to remove his coat, hung it in a closet, and invited him to sit down. "What do you want to drink?"

"Wine, scotch. Whatever you're having."

Richard knew Constance was testing him and refrained from looking around as if he were appraising her valuables. He kept his eyes strictly on her and made no comments, even about the exquisite marble fireplace right beside him.

At the bar, Constance studied the bottle Richard had brought, noticing for the first time that it was a special edition sealed with wax. Her expression made it clear she had no idea how to open it.

"Do you need help?" he asked.

"Maybe later." She abandoned the wine, poured two glasses of Chivas, and sat across from Richard.

"Cheers!" he said. "To whatever made you call me."

They both took sips of their drinks, and still mirroring Richard's smile, Constance said, "I'd like to apologize for that bullshit about money. I meant no offense."

"None taken."

Constance dried her glass and said, "This is hard for me, and I know I may regret this. But I like you, and you seem to like me, so I'll tell you why I was being weird when we went to bed." She got up. "Rather, I'll show you."

# 5

EYES AT THE wall above the couch where Richard sat, Constance started unbuttoning her blouse. Her head was so light she thought she might faint.

As Richard waited, he tried to guess which kind of deformity a wealthy woman had not been able to repair.

Finally, Constance opened her blouse, revealing a thin scar running from her right collar bone to the base of her left ribs. Her breasts seemed to melt down her chest, their nipples facing opposite poles.

"There," she said weakly. "Now you know why we can't date. Can you imagine, the plastic surgeon and the woman with unfixable boobs?"

"Constance."

"Please don't pretend you don't care. I heard my own father say a man couldn't fuck a woman with rotten breasts."

*Her dad's a real prick.* "What I meant to say was, this may be fixable."

Constance made a sound between laughter and a sob. "No, it can't. I saw dozens of doctors."

"Can I examine you?"

"God, no! I'm not consulting with you, I just wanted to show you why intimacy makes me uncomfortable."

"I'm a doctor, Constance. This doesn't scare me."

"Maybe not in the operating room. What about in your bed?"

"I want to help you. Please tell me what happened."

"No. This was more than enough. If we can change the subject, I'll try to get through dinner and enjoy your company. Otherwise, I'll ask you to please leave."

Richard lay back on the couch. "No and no."

"What?"

"No for changing the subject, and I'm not letting you go again. I'm in love with you."

Constance felt the rug under her feet begin to swallow her. Happiness was an occasional guest she never trusted. Suddenly her body became very heavy and she sat down, resting her head against her knees.

A moment later, Richard's hand was on her shoulder, then she sensed him kneeling in front of her. Constance was too frightened to open her eyes and Richard didn't force her to. He wrapped his arms around her and patiently waited until she looked at him again.

Their faces were very close, and Constance put her forehead against Richard's. "I fell into a fountain under construction when I was eleven and arrived at the ER with an iron rod impaled in my chest." She held his hand and asked him to sit beside her. It would be easier to tell her story without looking at him.

"There were four broken ribs and the doctors had to repair my stomach and one of my lungs. They said it was a miracle I survived."

"It truly was."

"Yes, but trying to save a child's life, they forgot what would happen in case she lived. The way they put my chest together was so messy my breasts couldn't develop. I had three surgeries after the initial one. One to create space for my breasts, and two others to correct the cosmetic problems. As you saw, none of them worked."

"May I ask you when your last surgery was done?"

"About eight years ago."

Richard nodded. "I'm begging you to believe that a lot has changed in the past years and there are other options."

Constance was calmer and she appreciated Richard's concern. Even if he was wrong. "Thank you, darling, but I have conformed."

"No you haven't. You pushed me away because you were ashamed. You're missing out, Constance."

"I'll never volunteer to another surgery. I can't."

"Would you agree to one consultation?"

"What for? The doctors told me my chest can't sustain my breasts in a symmetrical position. They tried everything!"

"They tried everything available then. And you tried every doctor here. The one I have in mind is in Brazil."

"Brazil? Oh, Richard. I heard of people losing their breasts doing augmentation in Mexico!"

"I know how it sounds and I had your same reaction. Have you heard of Niki Lauda, the race pilot who got badly burned in a crash?"

"Yes, I heard of the accident years ago when I was in Europe. Did he go to this doctor?"

"Mm-hmm. Lauda could have chosen anyone. He went to plastic surgeons in Germany, England, France, and settled for Dr. Pitanguy in Rio. Lauda calls him a genius and an artist, and I agree."

"I don't know... "

"Pitanguy gave a lecture at Harvard last year and I had the chance to talk to him about his techniques. You have the money, Constance. Go see him."

Richard's care and intelligence injected an unfamiliar warmth in Constance's veins. Something strange and delicious she would dare call hope.

She placed a hand on Richard's cheek. "I'm in love with you too."

When they went to bed this time there was no pretense. Lying on her back with Richard beside her, Constance said, "I still need to keep my blouse on."

"Whatever makes you comfortable. Just be fully here with me."

Constance nodded and Richard positioned himself on top of her. His elbows and knees sustaining his weight, he kissed her mouth and gently allowed his chest to touch hers. Constance gasped at the unusual contact, a mix of good and bad emotions she tried to tame.

Richard retreated a little and looked at her face. Even though her eyes were wet, she was smiling. She pulled him closer and this time allowed herself to enjoy every inch of his sensuous embrace. Richard was the right man for her, and she would never let him go.

# 6

RICHARD VISITED CONSTANCE'S apartment multiple times that week. They made love and discussed the details of sending her to Rio for an evaluation. He examined her and realized that a few weeks or months after each surgery, her implants proved too heavy for Constance's damaged chest, so they'd moved, which is why they started to look deformed.

Only by helping and encouraging her Richard noticed that Constance was putting her defenses down and falling hopelessly in love with him. If the surgery succeeded, which he trusted it would, Constance's family would possibly support their relationship. Or at least respect him enough to recommend him to valuable clients. Perhaps the Carltons even knew a prestigious clinic that could hire him. Richard was already happy with that prospect when Constance's case unexpectedly turned into his golden ticket.

Richard's free time was scarce that day, and he asked Constance to come have lunch with him near the hospital. "I talked to Pitanguy on the phone, and based on those photos I sent him, he's optimistic that he'll be able to perform a successful surgery."

Constance covered her face with both hands. "My gosh! Is this real?"

"I told you he was a genius. He just wants to examine you to be absolutely sure. If he decides to go for it, he'll do it in two phases, and you'll need a lot of down time there to recover."

"Are you sure you can't come with me at least for this initial consultation?"

"Nothing would make me happier. The problem is that I'll lose an entire semester of my program if I step away now."

Constance nodded. "I understand. My mom will come and stay for as long as I need her. I'd just feel better if you were there."

"Me too, and if we're a bit crazy, there may be a way."

"What?"

Richard laughed.

"You're giving me a heart attack. Tell me!"

"Pitanguy has a world-class surgeon's program in his hospital. If you want me to stay there with you, he said he'll take me."

"That would be marvelous! You love his work, and we'd kill two birds."

"It would be a dream. The problem is that I can only transfer back here if I complete a six-month program in Rio. You'll probably need only two or three months there, so it doesn't make sense."

Constance leaned forward and whispered, "You're fulfilling my dream. Can I play rich girl and help you fulfill yours?"

Sitting in her comfortable studio overlooking the pool, Victoria Carlton painted the final strokes on the still life she'd been working on for a month. A vase with the prettiest tiger lilies her garden had ever produced. Those prize-winning beauties were now gone except for a petal she kept among the pages of her planner. The painting did them justice and would be a lovely reminder.

Victoria did not allow the telephone to invade her creative space. The maid knocked almost fearfully and said, "Hate to disturb you, ma'am. Your daughter said it's important."

Victoria laughed inside. Everything was life or death for Constance. Being a level-headed woman who never lost control and kept a firm grip on her emotions, Victoria hated that her daughter's accident and its aftermath had made her so weak. Pushing thirty, Constance was still a child, and her motherly duty was to take care of her.

"Hello, sweetheart! How have you been?" Victoria sat down, expecting the usual long call.

"You won't believe it, Mom!" First Constance told Victoria about Pitanguy and her plans to attempt one more cosmetic surgery in Brazil.

"Connie, there's no way you're going to South America to have surgery without me."

"Thank you, Mom, but this time I won't need your help. I'm dating a plastic surgeon from Harvard. He's coming with me." Constance told her mother how she met Richard, how intelligent and kind he was, and that he would be perfect to take care of her.

Now Victoria was truly worried. She phrased her words carefully. "I'm elated, darling. For both things. Just to give me peace of mind, I'd like to ask you something."

When Timothy Carlton talked to you, you felt like you had been transported to the North Pole. Everything about the man was cold: his voice, his attitude, his pale blue eyes. Born and raised a millionaire, Constance's father could have spent his days among his dear horses and golf courses. That would have been a tremendous loss for their family business. Timothy was gifted with the mind of a mathematician, and was an effective strategic thinker. His weakness was dealing with people. He did well enough in social events among those he called *their people*, and by that he meant wealthy, white Republicans. He had no filter for anything else and his excessive objectivity often caused trouble, especially with his only daughter, whose sensitivities were beyond Timothy's grasp.

His wife, Victoria, was across the table telling him the news about Constance's upcoming surgery and new boyfriend.

"I need you to promise me, Tim, no matter the result of this surgery or whatever happens with this man, you'll shut your mouth."

Timothy remembered Victoria's almost divorcing him after Constance's attempted suicide, allegedly because of his comments. He would risk neither outcome again. "Of course, darling. I won't say a word."

Victoria sighed and sipped her tea. "This is a shitty situation, and we need to be smart about it. If this man has convinced Connie to go to the jungle to do something she was terrified about, God only knows what else he can do."

"You know my opinion about this. All that money spent on shrinks and our daughter still can't think straight when it comes to men."

"Well, she's too old for us to lock her in her room, so I'm going to Boston to meet this one. At least we'll know who we're dealing with."

"Want me to come with you?"

"I'm a better actor than you, my love. He'll be more comfortable showing his true colors if I go alone."

Timothy's shoulders relaxed. In the past years, being around Constance was like walking on a frozen lake that could unexpectedly break under his feet. He would give his right arm for her to have been born a boy.

"I can't believe Mom's here! I'm so excited!" No longer self-conscious of her naked body around Richard, Constance had adopted the habit of leaving the bathroom door open and talking to him from the shower.

Richard hated having to scream back for her to hear him. "Yes! Nice of her to come!"

Constance continued to blabber, and Richard focused on the full-length mirror in his bedroom. He inspected his hair, nails, and impeccably shaven face as if he had a mental checklist and was used to that process. He fixed the knot of his tie and, satisfied, opened his closet.

The Hermès scarf he'd so proudly bought as a teenager was now a vintage item he would no longer wear. Still, it remained in his wardrobe as a luck charm Richard playfully wrapped around his neck before important occasions. That first investment to become a wealthy man had brought him this far. Tonight, he would meet a possible obstacle to his plans with Constance, and to seduce her mother he had to be perfect.

"You're ready!" Constance was standing at the door, her wet hair twisted up in a towel.

Richard smiled. "I guess I'm excited too."

"You seem more nervous than excited. I've been talking to you and you're miles away."

"I'm a bit nervous. What if she hates me?"

"Mom's a sweetheart. You'll love each other."

They would meet at the elegant and ridiculously expensive Chateau Blanc restaurant, and Constance tactfully said, "Baby, you've been spending too much money on me. Let me handle this dinner."

"Absolutely not."

"I know you want to, but you can't afford that kind of stuff every weekend."

"You're worth it, even if I starve the rest of the month."

Behind Richard's playful air, Constance saw a thick layer of dignity and she felt safe she had finally met a decent man. "I love you!"

"I love you too."

Victoria was elegant in a southern, old-dame fashion. When Constance introduced them, instead of a handshake, Richard brought Victoria's hand to his lips. "I'm honored to meet you, Mrs. Carlton."

"The honor is mine, Richard. I can see why my daughter is so taken by you. Handsome and a gentleman."

"Thank you, ma'am. Like your daughter, you are very gracious."

"Please call me Victoria."

They sat down and Richard said, "Ladies, should we start with champagne?"

Under Victoria's disguised scrutiny, Richard talked to the waiter about the wine list and the menu with the confidence of one who routinely frequented those types of places.

"Do you speak French?" Victoria asked him.

"A little. But I'm a food and wine enthusiast. I can speak any languages that lead me to those."

Everyone laughed and Constance added, "He's being modest, Mom. Richard's French is pretty decent, and he speaks fluent Dutch."

"Really?" Victoria asked. "Have you lived abroad?"

"No. My father's family is from Rotterdam, and he taught me the language so I could stay in touch with my folks there. When I was growing up, my father and I visited every summer. My uncle had a sailboat, and my cousins were rowing aficionados. It was a lot of fun."

"Sounds like it!" said Victoria. "Do you still travel often?"

"Not since medical school. It's a heavy load. Last time I went to Europe my father was still alive."

"Oh, sorry to hear he's not around. What about your mother?"

"Not a good topic, Mom," Constance half whispered.

"Sorry." Victoria offered a sweet smile. "I didn't mean to put you on the spot, Richard."

"It's okay. If Constance doesn't mind listening to some of these stories again."

More fine Bordeaux was served as Richard told Victoria everything the mother of a rich woman would like to know about her daughter's suitor. That included the truth about whatever she could discover if she paid someone to investigate his past... and the untraceable lies he often fed her daughter.

After smoothing the trauma of his mother's abandonment with tales about the wonderful grandmother who replaced her, Richard fast-forwarded to his adolescence. "My father saw patients and taught at Columbia

University until I was seventeen. That year, he got a great proposal to teach at Harvard and we moved to Cambridge. That made my choice of college very easy."

Victoria did her best to catch Richard in a contradiction or any kind of statement that sounded fake or rehearsed. What she found was a strong, intelligent young man who had all the traits one needed to become successful. Maybe her prayers had finally been answered.

It wasn't until dessert that Victoria asked about Constance's surgery and their trip to Brazil, and Richard patiently described the process and answered her questions.

Victoria noticed the enamored way Constance looked at Richard. With their millions, she and Timothy could never fix their daughter. Physically or mentally. Now this man, with his confidence, knowledge, and hopefully love, had brought Constance back to life. Back to smiling.

Victoria felt both happy and sorry for her daughter. If the poor thing fell from that height, she wouldn't break; she would die. And yet, at that point, there was no safety net. Victoria decided the best she could do was act like an ally. Perhaps if Richard's life was happy and comfortable beside her daughter, the man would stay.

Back home, Richard was content with his performance. Dealing with Victoria Carlton had been a lot easier than he'd anticipated. She was intelligent in the way he thought wealthy folks were. They went to the right schools, knew influential people, and of course, great things happened to them. It was so effortless though; they went through life lacking the backbone of those who had to fight for what they wanted.

If he stuck to his script and good behavior, she shouldn't be a problem.

# 7

Rio de Janeiro was a feast for all senses. The constant pleasant weather, the shushing of palm trees dancing in the breeze. Beaches and parks surrounded by baroque architecture and street markets smelling of coconut and passion fruit. Everywhere under those vast blue skies, there were friendly, beautiful people with big hair and skin shades from golden tan to dark brown.

Richard and Constance arrived on a Friday and spent the weekend relaxing at the Copacabana Palace. On Monday, Richard accompanied his now official girlfriend to Dr. Pitanguy's local office for the evaluation. In the car he squeezed her hand. "Nervous?"

"Very, but in a good way."

Richard could say the same about himself. When Pitanguy had visited Harvard, Richard was enchanted by the man and believed his ground-breaking techniques could be a substantial differentiator for any plastic surgeon operating the United States.

Going to Brazil to learn from the master, however, seemed out of the question, even for a high achiever like him. The best Richard had managed in the occasion was to befriend Dr. Paulo Correa, a fellow plastic surgeon on Pitanguy's team who accompanied the famous doctor on his trip to America.

Richard had shown Correa the best of Harvard, and the two later enjoyed beers on a tour around Boston. They had been in touch since then, and Correa had been instrumental to Richard in the past weeks. Richard made a mental note to buy the man a nice bottle of wine.

Constance's eyes were on the exotic sidewalk of Copacabana Beach, a mosaic of black and white stones in the shape of waves. She sensed Richard's eyes and smiled. He pretended to share her interest outside the window. When she looked away again, his eyes remained on her.

Constance's hair was up, like the first time they went to bed, and Richard contemplated the long road they had traveled in mere weeks. That night he'd been gambling. Now, they had a perfect win-win relationship. He didn't even have to feel guilty.

The consultation was at Dr. Pitanguy's private clinic in Botafogo, where he operated on his VIP clientele. According to Richard's new best friend, Dr. Correa, celebrities and even royalty secretly came to that clinic, and among the jet set, the expression "going to Brazil on vacation" was becoming synonymous with "having work done by Pitanguy."

While in theory Richard was there for Constance, he couldn't wait to see Dr. Pitanguy in action.

As jovial and welcoming as Richard remembered him, Pitanguy stood up when he and Constance entered his office and shook their hands. After warmly greeting Richard, Pitanguy told Constance, "Ms. Carlton, I'm honored you're considering doing this surgery with me. Please follow my nurse and I'll be with you shortly."

"Can Richard join us for the consultation?"

"Of course."

While Constance changed, Pitanguy discussed his initial ideas with Richard, then the two doctors joined Constance in the examination room.

After he'd studied the tissues of Constance's chest and breasts, Pitanguy explained why previous surgeries had failed and what he would do to prevent it from reoccurring. "I understand you've been through an enormous ordeal," he told Constance. "And if you need time to consider it, please don't feel obligated."

Constance was sold. She looked at Richard, who nodded, and she told Pitanguy, "Let's do it as soon as you're available."

That was an afternoon of celebration for Richard and Constance, with plenty of champagne and lovemaking. Around seven that evening, a golden veil invaded their room and quickly began to fade. From their bed, they looked outside the floor-to-ceiling windows and the sun was dissolving in the ocean, allowing its smaller sisters to shine in the dark skies. Everything looked and felt like a dream, and Constance wished she could immortalize that moment in a painting she could admire every single day.

That week they rented an apartment in Ipanema, and while Constance did her preoperative tests, Richard was introduced to Pitanguy's program for surgeons.

The private clinic had the usual cosmetic cases: facelifts, breast augmentation and reduction, liposuction; and young surgeons did a considerable part of their training there. Richard was excited when Pitanguy said his six-month program would be split between his private clinic and the public hospital, where the brilliant doctor offered free cosmetic and reconstructive surgeries to individuals without means.

Pitanguy believed there was a transformative effect in a surgeon who learned how to deal with the disfigured. Decades earlier, he'd been one of the few Brazilian experts in the reconstruction of severely burned skin. He became famous after operating on dozens of fire victims in a circus tent, many of them children.

In his first class, Pitanguy said, "Everyone has a right to beauty, and part of our mission as plastic surgeons is to change the idea that cosmetic surgery is vanity. If someone has a terrible nose or a scar that makes them feel ashamed, that should be treated as remedial operations, like cleft palates and burns. Because if we fix them, we're also healing a psychological ailment."

Richard loved his first week of studies at the public hospital. The doctors spoke English and he could catch up on what he observed with his colleagues' translations.

While the practice was as intensive as at Beth Israel, the experience was much richer. The enormous cultural hiatus between life in South America and in the United States brought cases Richard would have never seen in his country.

People showed up at the hospital with faces disfigured by razors, and Dr. Paulo Correa explained, "Some men in lower-income populations have razor fights."

"Like a duel?" Richard asked.

"Yeah. Only not always until death. One man may dress up in his finest suit and never return home. Another may cower halfway through the fight and end up here." Correa sobered. "With women, it's more unfair. If they've got a razor scar on their face, it's likely someone marked them as a prostitute."

It was fascinating.

Richard enjoyed the work so much he could have lived in that hospital happily absorbing knowledge and experience. A shame that Constance was financing the tour and that he'd need to go home and play boyfriend. Richard's only disappointment was that Pitanguy wouldn't allow him to watch any of

Constance's surgeries.

"It's not a good idea, Richard. I know you want to

be there for her, but if something goes wrong, you'll be in our way to save her life."

If Pitanguy only knew. Medically, Constance's case was so uncommon, Richard desperately wanted to watch Pitanguy's magical scalpel fixing her. If she died, it would merely be an inconvenience. "I understand, Doctor. Would you allow me to do my credits at the clinic during her surgeries so at least I'll be around when she's done?"

"Of course."

Constance's first surgery happened on their second week in Rio. When she awoke slightly groggy from anesthesia, she found Richard sitting beside her.

"I love your eyes," she said. "They're strong and sweet, like you."

Richard smiled. His eyes were as much a chameleon as he was. Not clear blue like his father's or brown like his mother's. A flexible hazel that went darker or brighter according to the lights. "They can't get enough of you," he said.

"Good. Soon, they'll have something pretty to look at."

Richard worked long hours and Constance stayed at the clinic for several days.

When she was ready to go home, Richard hired English-speaking nurses and a local assistant to run their house.

"You're an angel," Constance said.

*Enjoy it while it lasts.* "I wish I could stay home and take care of you full-time."

"Then who will do my plastic surgeries when I get old?"

"Not me. I wouldn't be allowed to perform surgery on my wife."

Constance's smile would have illuminated a small town.

It was hard for Constance to look at herself flat-chested. Her hope lay on the fact that Pitanguy had done what other plastic surgeons hadn't. Before the actual aesthetic procedures, he removed all the scar tissue and repaired the base of her chest.

Almost two months after the initial surgery, the final wraps were off and Constance could see her chest muscles in the right place, her skin smooth, its color homogeneous. "Now, with a solid chest and healthy muscles, you're ready for me to build you perfect breasts." Pitanguy smiled. "This time, they will stay in place."

"I trust you, Doctor, I just can't help being afraid."

"Don't be. If I had any doubts it wouldn't work, I wouldn't put you through this."

Pitanguy exuded confidence and Constance believed him. She imagined Richard a decade later and could see him doing the same for a patient like her. He would become a marvelous doctor and she intended to do everything in her power to help him.

After three hours of surgery, Constance was taken to her room. She awoke in a surgical bra designed to shape the breasts and decrease the swelling. She was warned that this was far from the final results, but she cried at the substantial improvement she already saw. She had proportional C-cup breasts with nipples finally pointing in the same direction.

A prayer escaped her lips. "Please, keep them this way!"

Richard spent some time with Constance and shared her happiness as she called her parents in Houston.

"I need to go now," he said. "I'll be checking on you nonstop."

As he hit the corridor, Dr. Correa silently signaled for Richard to join him in an empty room. "What's up?" Richard asked as they closed the door.

"You can meet your first big celebrity today."

"Who?"

"Someone no one can know is having a nip tuck. She's here for a facelift and you'll see how it's done, so she can go home and pretend she just had a great night of sleep."

Richard's skin was tingling. He could see himself rising to Pitanguy's level one day. The celebrities coming. The millions accumulating in his bank account. Pitanguy performed five operations a day with the help of a few postgraduate students. The others watched from the clinic theater via closed-circuit TV. Richard was eager to get in. "I can't wait!"

"For this type of client, secrecy is key, and the boss

only allows one or two surgeon trainees in the room. He said if you don't tell anyone, including your fiancée, you can join us."

"I'll pretend I've never heard of this woman."

Correa laughed. "We make a good team, Wilken. Maybe you should move to Rio."

Richard and Correa went through the disinfection process, put on their masks, hats, and gloves, and entered Pitanguy's operating room. The anesthesiologist had already done his job and the very special patient was down. Richard couldn't possibly pretend he didn't know the woman. Her face was in half the movies his father watched since he was a kid.

A week later, another famous singer arrived from Europe. The following one, a member of royalty. Pitanguy was truly the "Michelangelo of the scalpel," as the media called him. Unlike other plastic surgeons, he didn't try to make someone look ten years younger. He made them look refreshed so no one could tell for sure if they'd had any work done. Some patients returned once a year and, with the master's subtle touch, remained ageless.

At that point, Constance was starting to believe this surgery had truly worked. For another forty-five days, she would have to wear the special bra and a strap around her chest for the implants to stay in place. She could not lift weights or raise her arms above her head. The nurse helped her bathe and get dressed, and her assistant handled whatever else she needed: finding an American magazine, renting a movie, going out for a walk.

With Richard away all day, six days a week, Constance was starting to get bored. Other than her staff, she knew no one in Rio and didn't speak the language. Despite the beautifully decorated apartment and the gorgeous views of the ocean right across the street, there was little to do. She couldn't go to the pool or the beach. Her fair skin burned easily, and after such major surgery, water or sun-bathing could be an invitation to infections or complications.

Constance spent her days reading or on the phone with her mother and friends. The best time of her day was when she removed the medical paraphernalia to take a shower and could admire her new breasts. Firm and pretty like they had been in her dreams. Sometimes Constance cried. Sometimes she laughed so hard the nurses seemed concerned. She began to develop a passionate notion of the miracles of plastic surgery.

One day, in front of the mirror, she studied her ass, her thighs, and even her just-turned-thirty-years-old face as if they were under a microscope. Maybe there were other parts of her body that could be improved. That was when Constance knew she would marry Richard, and she had to be patient for him to get the best out of his specialization.

He would always be beside her and would never let her be ugly again.

As he did at Harvard, Richard quickly raised to the top of his class in Rio, and Pitanguy loved him. They often spent time talking after the surgeries. That week, they had five high-caliber celebrities in town waiting for procedures. The poor souls had been followed by the media in and out of their hotels.

"It'll be impossible to get them to the clinic without being seen," Richard told Pitanguy.

"Don't worry. We'll figure it out."

"And what if the media asks if these people saw you?"

"I'll say they did, just not to have work done," Pitanguy said, laughing. "Richard, keeping your patients' privacy is as important as performing a great surgery. If they travel half the world to come see you and don't want paparazzi to know about it, you throw some parties and hang out with them socially."

Pitanguy was a celebrity himself. The Brazilian press chronicled his well-frequented charity dinners and the celebrities enjoying the tropical waters in his yacht or arriving by helicopter at his private island. Richard loved his new mentor. Pitanguy was not only teaching him how to be a better doctor. He was teaching him how to befriend the clientele who would make him a star.

Richard was dying to see Pitanguy's island. Sadly, the invitation never came. He was ready to ask Correa what the ticket price was for entering their mentor's inner circle when, during Constance's final consultation, Pitanguy said, "Now that you can enjoy the beach, my dear, I'd like you both to come to my home." He turned to Richard. "Just please don't mention it to your colleagues so they won't feel left out."

"Of course. Thank you!"

"*Vai ser ótimo!*" Constance said. "Did Richard tell you I'm learning Portuguese?"

"That's marvelous, darling. Will help you make friends."

Watching Pitanguy and Constance laugh as old friends, Richard liked to believe his mentor had invited him because he was his smartest apprentice. And yet, he was aware that even if that was the case, Pitanguy might have also invited him because of who his girlfriend was.

Even though Richard had no intention of spending his life with Constance, it seemed time to promote her to the wife category and benefit from the doors her family name could open. He decided to meet Timothy Carlton as soon as they returned to the United States and start seducing the real gatekeeper of their fortune.

# 8

THE NEXT MONTHS until the end of Richard's program passed like nothing he had previously experienced. Both too fast, like a beautiful landscape flashing by a train window, and as a lifetime in a magical place where each day was rich and adventurous.

Richard and Constance attended brunches and parties at Pitanguy's island, and Constance spent entire weeks as a guest there while Richard worked. They couldn't get enough of it. One day by the beach, with an audience of blue birds watching them, Constance said, "I wanna move to Rio."

Richard chuckled. "I wanna fly to the moon."

"I'm serious. For me, this isn't just an exotic place. It's where I became my best self and people meet me as Constance, not poor Connie or the heir of the Carltons. Please, Richard, don't you love it here too?"

Richard did, but that seat was taken. He wanted to go somewhere he could be the plastic surgeon who offered new skills and techniques. Back in the U.S., he would have a differentiator. Here, he would disappear under Pitanguy's shadow. "Darling, I do love it here. It just doesn't feel like home."

"I don't like it back home."

"You didn't like it with your old life. Your old problems. Look at you now! You're gorgeous and we're together. We can build any life we want."

She considered. "I like that. But we could be happy here too. Get a beautiful house by the beach. Make new friends. Pitanguy loves you. I'm sure he would hire you."

*How narrow-minded.* "Darling, that wasn't our plan. How about we go back home, I finish my program and you give me a year or two to get my bearings? If things don't work, we'll talk about it again."

"So, you do see us together in a year or two?"

"At least a decade or two."

Constance hugged him. "Deal. But we have to come back on vacation."

"Any time you want."

On the last day of Richard's program, Pitanguy was talking about a complex hand surgery and Richard told Dr. Correa, "I'll miss him."

"Yeah, famous doctors like to elevate their knowledge by making things seem difficult. He makes everything easy for us."

A few days before their departure, Constance threw a dinner in their Ipanema apartment to honor Dr. Ivo Pitanguy and his wife. Dr. Correa and a few of their closest colleagues were also present.

When everyone was at the table, Constance raised her glass and said, "You've changed my life, Ivo. Not only my body. Thank you!"

Her blond curls framing her face, Constance looked angelic and happier than ever. With her new breasts, she seemed to have gained a new brain. No more complexes, no more hidden parts. She was a full woman and maybe, she thought, she could finally be loved, regardless of her bank account.

When the guests left, Constance told Richard to wait ten minutes and meet her in the bedroom. "I have a surprise."

She was wearing a sensuous nightgown with cleavage almost to her belly button. "Wow!" Richard said. "That's what I call showing off one's assets."

That felt like winning the Miss Universe pageant for Constance. Her cheeks almost hurt from the extension of her smile. Despite her resistance and fears, that man had seen the best of her, brought it to the surface, and made her shine. No one had ever made her feel so worthy, and she wanted him around for the rest of her life.

"I brought us champagne," Richard said. "Let's drink to your beauty."

Constance came closer. "I may have something better to celebrate. Will you marry me?"

The Carltons hated the news about the engagement. Richard had no fortune or pedigree and had been dating their daughter less than a year. Victoria had met him once and Timothy had only spoken to him on the phone. What shocked them the most was that it never occurred to Constance to consult with them about something so serious. She simply called and said, "Mom, Dad, I know you won't approve, but Richard and I are getting married."

Timothy's face turned red, and Victoria signaled to him not to make a sound. "That's big news, honey. I'm sure you thought a lot about it."

"I did, Mom. Richard is a solid man who makes me feel safe. I'm no longer a deformed woman, and I believe he actually loves me."

"Don't talk like that, darling. You're beautiful and of course he loves you. He already did before the surgery."

"So, you support my decision?"

"Of course! We're happy for you."

After a suspicious pause, Constance asked, "Are you listening to this, Dad?"

Timothy kept his eyes on Victoria. "I am, honey, and I agree with your mother. Richard is certainly a problem solver, and he seems to be making you happy."

"Incredibly happy."

"So, you have our blessings."

Victoria produced a fake laughter of excitement. "Congratulations, sweetheart! Please make plans to bring Richard here so we can welcome him to the family."

When Constance hung up, Timothy told Victoria, "At least this one is a doctor. I think we'll have to swallow this engagement and hope for the best."

Victoria nodded. "Connie's self-esteem is very fragile and she needs our support. Besides, I have to admit Richard seems legit. Not many conmen have escaped my radar."

"It's a reliable radar. If you approve of him, he can't be so bad."

"Well, my approval will come with time. For now, let's say he's on probation."

Richard and Constance returned to the States in mid-August and flew to Houston soon afterward for a weekend celebrating their engagement. On Saturday, a hundred people attended the elegant brunch party in the family's mansion. In the next twenty-four hours, Constance and Richard hung out with the family's inner circle. Everyone loved Richard, and even Timothy was pleasantly surprised.

The snobbish old man had narrow ideas about the middle class and tended to envision what he called "regular folks" as poorly dressed beer drinkers who watched football on TV and threw barbecue parties in their backyards. His daughter's fiancé might be financially below her, but he walked, talked, and dressed like one of them.

Richard felt at home discussing art and collectibles

with Timothy and Victoria. He was not intimidated by a fancy table with fifty types of glasses and silverware, and he could pick and explain the highlights of the most exquisite wines.

At heart, Richard was a Democrat. Out of convenience, he had remained neutral about politics his entire life, so in a moment like now, he could claim to be a passionate Republican. Not that skillful at golf, Richard's smart political remarks kept Timothy and his friends entertained while they played.

When they were saying goodbyes to return to Boston, Timothy said, "I'm very impressed by you, Richard. You are a refined young man."

"Thank you, Mr. Carlton. My father taught me the value of a diverse education."

"He must have been proud."

Back at her Boston home that evening, Constance told Richard, "We should move to Houston after the wedding."

Houston was in the center of two plastic surgery meccas: Beverly Hills and Miami. Since Richard had met Constance, the idea had crossed his mind. "I thought you wanted to stay here," he said.

"Well, Houston makes more sense now. That city belongs to my family. We own important real estate and know everyone who matters. You can have your own clinic and clients who'll make you famous."

"Sounds wonderful. My concern after what you told

me is that your parents will think less of me if we start our life with their money."

Constance looked at her fiancé tenderly. "You're nothing like the other men in my life. And we wouldn't need their approval. Grandma left me all her money. We can do whatever we want."

Richard couldn't sleep that night. He had done his part of the bargain and the universe was delivering the rest. Houston was the place he would build his kingdom.

# BOSTON

———

## BACK TO JANUARY 1986

# 9

TWO YEARS SINCE Richard had first set foot in Constance's elegant townhouse, seeing her was far from exciting. She had grown moody and childish, and he stayed with her out of willpower, envisioning his dream clinic feeding the Houston nobility.

Of course, a couple of years into their marriage, when he had made a name for himself and accumulated enough wealth, Richard intended to divorce her.

Keeping their separate homes until the wedding was a tremendous relief to him, and extremely convenient when he and Sally Landry discovered they could be more than colleagues.

Richard had been careful not to raise Constance's suspicions about his faithfulness. After gaining her trust, his schedule at the hospital became whatever he decided to tell her. With Sally's murder, however, his whereabouts the night of the murder might be investigated, and he needed to ensure that he and Constance were on the same page.

What he told the police was close to the truth. Constance had been at the museum gala, and she'd indeed thought Richard had gone home to catch up on sleep. But she had been busy in the past two weeks, and they had only spoken over the phone. Richard wanted to see Constance tonight and have the bases covered.

"Hello, beautiful!" Richard said when Constance opened the door.

"Hey."

"It's been too long. I miss you!" He hugged her and Constance's arms remained limp by her side. Richard stepped back and took a better look at her face. "What's wrong?"

"I didn't sleep much last night."

"Sorry to hear that. Still want to go out?"

"I have a better idea. Come on in."

Richard grinned. "Sounds promising." He removed his coat and made his way to the leather chair by the fireplace. That evening, he wished he could stitch his cheeks up to sustain his fake smile. Playing a character 24/7 was exhausting. With Sally, he could talk about what he wanted and fuck as he liked. To endure the first years of his marriage, he would definitely need another Sally.

Constance sat on the couch across from him. "Janette cooked us dinner so we could stay in and talk."

"Sounds perfect." Richard was extremely attentive to Constance. He kept a smile on his face while inquiring about her boring fundraising events; sounded excited about their wedding plans; and, the toughest one, seemed passionate in bed, even though compared to Sally, Constance felt like an inflatable doll. "Why didn't you sleep, sweetheart, any problems at the gala?"

"No. I know about you and Sally Landry."

Richard felt like a bucket of cold water had been thrown on his face. *No. And not now.* He tried to think fast, to make up a reasonable story. His brain unapologetically failed him. He had exhausted his improvisation skills with Detective Berman.

"You don't deny it?" she asked.

*Too late for that.* "Lying would be worse than omitting. I guess I can only apologize."

Constance shook her head. "Sixth sense is a bitch. I remember her from the last hospital event we attended. Beautiful brunette. Not many women can pull off either a tight white gown or ear-length hair. But that woman had a killer body, and her haircut only emphasized her perfect jaws."

Sally was not the goddess in Constance's recollection and that concerned Richard.

Constance went on talking. "I was jealous when you spoke to her that evening. I sensed some electricity between you. Then her husband joined us, and I felt safe." She laughed. "What a fool I was. Never thought of her again until I saw you together by the subway station."

"You're not a fool. Sally and I were working

83

together several nights in a row, and we made a bad call. I never meant to hurt you, and if you can give me another chance, I'll do anything you want. We can even move back to Brazil if that's still your dream."

"That's quite generous."

"Anything for you."

"And leaving the country now would be to make me happy or because you killed her?"

Richard jumped from his chair. "Constance!"

"Stay where you are." Low as it was, her voice had the power of martial law.

Richard obeyed, uncertain of what would hit him next. "I didn't kill anyone."

"You've been acting pretty cold for someone who's just lost his lover."

"I didn't love her! I was shocked when I heard the news, but that was nothing I would bring to you."

"I'm sure the police would be intrigued. Especially since you were at Sally's place last night."

"Did you follow me?"

"No darling, rich girls pay people to do that kind of thing. I have tons of photos of you two."

It was the first time Richard recalled experiencing true fear. The type one must feel when attacked by a wild animal or, more in this context, while waiting his turn on death row. Fear stung his tongue with its bitter taste, and he had no idea what to say. *Breathe.* "What do you want, Constance?"

"How about what you asked me the first time we

went to bed?" Richard's expression was blank, and Constance filled the gap. "Honesty and respect."

"Oh, cut the riddles! What the fuck do you want?"

"Nice to meet you, stranger. I guess that's the real you."

"I'm sorry," Richard said, his voice tamed again. "I know betraying you was very wrong, and you have every right to be mad. But do you understand that bringing up my involvement with Sally now will ruin my life?"

"I sure do."

"And is it worth it? Losing everything we have to punish me?"

"And everything we have is what exactly?"

"Our love, our marriage."

"My money?"

"I don't care about your money. I just want a second chance."

"Are you sure about that?"

Richard hated where that conversation was heading. "Of course."

"Very well then. Wait here."

Richard couldn't stay still. He went to the bar and served himself a double scotch. How Detective Berman would love that. He'd go straight to DNA testing and it would be a perfect match.

Richard drank half the contents of his glass and refilled it. How stupid he had been. How sentimental. He should have filled the bathtub with Clorox and sunk Sally's goddamned body in it!

The only upside of that mess was that if Constance had known about the affair, she or whoever she had paid to follow him might be the anonymous caller. That would be great. He wouldn't have to worry about that extra problem, and with the right talk, he might be able to keep the situation contained.

Constance was returning, her high heels against the floor the ominous sound of a judge's gavel preceding his verdict. "Please, sit here," she said, pointing at the couch. She sat beside Richard and opened a folder, spread different documents on the coffee table.

"A prenup and a confession?" Richard tried to be playful like they both did every time there was too much tension. He tried to look confident, but Constance knew tonight she had the upper hand.

She remained serious. "If you love me and want us to leave this behind, you'll sign these papers."

"What are they?"

"Everything I need to trust your good intentions. I still love you, Richard, but I no longer trust you. While I'm learning how to do it again, I want you to be in the same position."

Constance picked the first document that was attached to a deed. "This one regards your clinic. I already bought the building, and it would have been my surprise wedding present for you. With the new events, I talked to my lawyer, and we included an agreement to protect my interests, and honestly, my heart."

"Constance... "

"Please don't interrupt me with sentimentalities. Not good timing."

"Sorry. Go ahead."

"You can have the clinic and the funds you need to make it successful. But starting the day of our wedding, I will handle all our money, including what you'll make through the clinic."

"You're kidding me!"

"And if you cheat or divorce me, you'll leave with nothing."

"Wanna throw my left kidney on it too?"

"If you think this is unreasonable, let me ask you this. Did you tell the police you were with Sally last night?"

"Of course not! She was perfectly fine when I left. Why would I bring trouble to myself?"

"So, you cheated on me, lied to the police, and are asking me to trust you. You need to trust me as well."

"And if I say no?"

"We're done." Constance looked down at the paperwork. "My parents warned me about gold diggers my entire life and this will force me to admit that they were right about you. The invitations are already out, and canceling the wedding would be a terrible humiliation. You'd be ruining my life, Richard, and I don't give a shit about ruining yours." She slid the papers toward him and below them, Richard spotted the photos.

*Shit!* Constance's investigator was really good. Those weren't blurred images or innocent interactions Richard could dispute. The man had a professional camera able to capture clear shots of him and Sally making out in her car in a remote area near the airport, and some of the two furtively entering Sally's home from the back entrance. There were more photos under those. Richard didn't dare touch them.

Constance noticed where his eyes landed and said, "You can have these. I have copies in my safety deposit box."

Richard said nothing and Constance continued, "But if what you've done was a one-time mistake and we stay happily married, you won't even have to remember what's in this folder."

Richard had no intention of letting that bitch reduce him to a puppet. He was only temporarily cornered. Constance had become an immeasurable danger and he would play along until he found a safe way to get rid of her. "Fair enough," he finally said. "I have one condition."

"You have balls, Richard. You're in no position."

"It's not about money or anything you said. My condition is that if I accept your proposal, you won't see it as I succumbed to blackmail. Otherwise, we'll both live in hell."

"You deserve hell."

"But you don't, and despite your anger, you don't think I killed Sally, or you wouldn't be here with me."

"I don't know who you are anymore. I did everything for you to be mine and it failed. That's the best I could come up with to protect myself."

"My condition to sign this is that if I give up the money, your heart will remain open."

"I'll try."

"Not good enough."

"It's all I've got, Richard."

"So, I can't do it. There's no guarantee you won't wake up mad tomorrow and go to the police anyways."

"Will you take that chance?"

"So you *are* blackmailing me?"

"I just hope that with the right incentive, you'll become a better man."

"Okay, I'll bite if you do. Come to bed with me. Prove you still love me."

"Sleep on it, Richard. Tomorrow we'll make decisions." She paused. "About everything."

"No, you listen to me. I learned my lesson and I want to regain your trust. I'll sign your damned papers and I won't ever cheat on you again. But if you want revenge no matter what I do, I'll walk on eggshells for the rest of my life. If that's your game, I'll talk to the police myself."

Richard grabbed his coat and headed out, hoping Constance would call his bluff and come after him like in previous fights. She didn't. His hand was on the doorknob and she remained immobile.

*Now what? Turn around and surrender?* Richard was exhausted from tension and could not devise a better tactic. Uncertain, he left and shut the door.

He stood in the front yard, the cold air gradually bringing him some clarity. Constance was unstable and a deal with her could never involve only papers. He had always been able to manipulate her because she found him strong. Showing weakness now, even under pressure, would be a bad call. Better let things chill and touch base later before she went to bed.

Richard was at the gate when Constance called him. He turned around slowly, almost as if he shouldn't, and she rushed to him.

Arms around his waist, face buried in his chest, she whispered, "My heart is open."

Richard caressed Constance's back and as he did, every tense muscle in his body began to relax. He rested his chin on top of her head, and the long, empty street ahead seemed a reminder of the worth of freedom.

*This one was close, but I won.* He smiled.

# 10

CARVING HER WAY out of a nightmare in which her nose melted down her chin, Constance sat in bed panting. It took her a few seconds to get her bearings. The bed was still warm beside her. Richard had recently left for work, and traces of his elegant cologne lingered in the linens, causing her longing and pain.

Adjacent to the bed was a fireplace with a table and a duo of Chippendale chairs. Richard had signed the papers there after she made love to him and promised that their pact would grant them a clean slate.

*But would it?* When Constance learned about the affair, she became possessed by jealousy. She wasn't satisfied hiring an investigator to follow the cheating duo. Obsessed with discovering what made Sally better than her, Constance wanted a listening device installed in Sally's house.

"That's not easy," said the investigator, who was a former cop. "I've done it, but—"

"I'll pay you a hundred thousand dollars."

After weeks of listening to the recordings, Constance felt like she knew Sally Landry. The thirty-two-year-old doctor from Virginia was loud and fast, always multitasking. Sally listened to jazz while studying and did yoga twice a week. She hated pets and had mixed feelings about having children.

With their busy schedules, the Landrys had a life of excessive work and little pleasure. Monotonous and routine without serious signs of marital problems. When Sally was on the phone, Constance could only hear her side of the conversations. Chats were fun with her friends, health-focused with her mother, and sweet with her brother. Richard, of course, never called Sally's home.

The first time Constance heard his voice in a recording was during one of their dates in Sally's home, and she couldn't believe they were so bold. John Landry had left the house an hour earlier.

Richard and Sally rushed to bed, laughing, and Richard said, "Suck me!" Constance threw the ear sets on the desk, barely breathing, and stared at them, the muffled sound of lovemaking stabbing her chest. She returned to that recording later and catatonically sat there absorbing the torturous soundtrack.

When she was done, she called her lawyer and started crafting her prenuptial agreement. Constance asked her investigator to remove the device from Sally's place and just follow Richard until she was ready to confront him.

Constance only spoke to Richard on the phone during the two weeks preceding the museum gala. She wouldn't have had the strength to handle that enormous responsibility if she'd had to pretend everything was well between them.

As she found excuses not to meet him, Richard faked frustration. "We've been too busy these final months in Boston. I can't wait for our wedding!"

Constance would allow Richard to see Sally one more time and unmask him the night after the gala.

The evening of the museum event was agony. Constance kept imagining Richard in Sally's arms, then confronting him the following day. She felt foolish. She could break up with Richard or give him a second chance and hope for the best. But if he didn't love her, she had no power.

The charismatic MC presented the cause their organization was helping, and wealthy patrons began raising hands to donate money. Constance's mind was back at the thick envelope resting on her desk. She had read her lawyer's instructions, then random lines of the various documents he had sent her. The key words in the prenup and the other agreements were *funds, protection, penalty*. What a way to start a marriage, she thought.

Constance recalled the recordings of Richard and Sally. With Sally, his laughter was more authentic. His pleasure more intense.

A loud round of applause exploded in the ballroom, and the MC praised a million-dollar donation. Constance laughed. That's what she represented to Richard. His fundraising until he could make his own money. She took an extra Valium and an hour later seemed like a zombie parading among the guests.

Midway into dinner, the chairwoman of the art committee approached her. "Constance, are you all right?"

"Just a bit tired."

The woman studied Constance's face and, convinced that she was drugged, said, "You seem ill, sweetie. My driver will take you home."

Constance arrived home at nine thirty and almost called Richard out of habit. Instead, she went to her office and stared at the prenup and other agreements. Even if Richard signed those papers, she had nothing to truly keep him beside her. It would be a question of time until he left her or cheated again.

She carefully put the paperwork back in the envelope and threw it in the bin.

On the following morning, Constance had such a headache she was about to call in sick and tell Richard not to come that evening. The news from her investigator changed everything. "Sally Landry was murdered last night," the man said on the phone.

Constance grabbed the table for support. "Did Richard do it?"

"I don't know. They walked into her place around seven p.m. I'm familiar with the route he takes later and no longer wait for him. I wish I had last night." The investigator related the details of how Sally's home and body were found and said, "For now, your fiancé's not a suspect. I'll keep you posted. Just giving you the heads-up in case he's trickier than you expected."

With that turn of events, Constance had fished the paperwork out of the trash and confronted Richard with much more power. After their fight last night, she had no doubt that he was a lot trickier than expected, and yet, he was now in her hands.

She rang the maid to bring her breakfast in bed, and twenty minutes later, the woman knocked and walked in. "Good morning, ma'am. Same place as usual?"

Constance nodded.

Assuming that her boss's silence meant she was having her usual bad day, the maid set the table, poured a cup of fresh coffee, and left.

Constance reached for the drawer of her bedside table first and found the familiar bottles. She grabbed the largest one, opened it, and popped a Valium in her mouth. She could swallow it without water.

Slowly, she got up and glanced at her breakfast. A plate with smoked salmon, capers, and boiled eggs. Another with brown toast and French butter. Simultaneously hungry and nauseous, she sipped the coffee and headed to the other table, where the documents were.

Constance double-checked that none of the pages were missing Richard's signature and put the stack in the envelope that would be mailed to her lawyer in Houston. Too anxious to wait for news or even turn on the TV, she called her investigator.

He said, "All the neighbors were interrogated yesterday, and no one saw anything. As usual, the husband is the first suspect the police have to eliminate."

Constance had watched the news the day before, and she couldn't make up her mind about John Landry. He had appeared on TV sobbing, his vivid pain an alibi almost as strong as the dozen witnesses testifying that he was at work until he received the anonymous call.

"Do you know what he told the cops?" Constance asked.

"According to one of my colleagues, John Landry said only wonderful things about his wife. He didn't even hint they had any issues, much less that she was cheating."

"Strange. Richard and Sally were fucking inside the man's home. Do you think he really didn't know?"

The investigator chuckled. "Some men are truly clueless. Others, smart enough to play dumb."

It didn't make sense to Constance that she knew about the affair and John Landry didn't.

The investigator continued, "In my line of work, I've seen dangerous men who look like choir boys. If John Landry intended to kill his wife with his bare hands, as many cheated men do, he may have paid someone to place that call."

"Why?"

"To give him a reason to go home and still have a decent alibi."

"What about the time of death?"

"Well, that's his specialty." The investigator laughed. "I found out that John Landry is a pathologist."

"No shit?"

"Yeah. He definitely knew his wife enjoyed alcohol and drugs, and that they affect the estimated time of death. Hers had a three-hour window, which means that the killer could have been your fiancé, Landry, or a random intruder."

Constance couldn't picture Richard strangling Sally or staging a crime scene. What she was worried about was the anonymous caller. When Richard asked if she had been the one who called John Landry that night, Constance found herself nodding.

Why complicate things by revealing the anonymous letter she'd received a month earlier telling her about the affair? Pushing Richard to sign those papers would only be possible if he thought she was his only threat.

Now, if the anonymous caller was the same person who sent her the letter, he or she knew both Constance and John Landry and wanted their cheating partners to get caught.

Since her investigator had also been a detective with the Boston PD, Constance asked his opinion, and he said, "If Landry arranged that anonymous call, that's the reason he only called the police after he got home, not when he left his job."

"And no one found it suspicious?"

"That's when the anonymous call worked in his favor. Landry claimed he wanted to check if the call was a prank before bothering the cops. He was interrogated and tested of course, but his body exhibited no signs of fighting, and the semen found in the victim wasn't his."

Constance trembled at the possibility of Richard becoming a suspect. After a long sigh, she said, "Richard told me that Sally was asleep when he left. Assuming he's telling the truth, his prints were definitely on the crime scene, and possibly his semen. If someone saw him and didn't show up yet, they may be planning to blackmail Richard or me."

"That's possible. And you should start thinking about how involved you wanna be if that happens."

"What choices do I have?"

"If this explodes, your fiancé is the one to blame. You'll only be in trouble if the caller blackmails you and you don't tell the police."

"Which would mean admitting to the cops that Richard was there."

"Sad as it is, it would be the only way for you not to become an accomplice. You could be in the wrong just by knowing about his affair with the victim and not coming forward."

"And if John Landry killed Sally, do you think he might have sent me the letter to turn me into a second suspect in case the police discovered the affair?"

"Possibly. You'd be the other cheated partner potentially interested in revenge."

"That's what I thought."

"Well, for now, I recommend you sit still. If someone reaches out to you, let me handle them."

Constance's voice came out as a murmur. "Okay."

"And as a precaution, should I continue to keep an eye on your fiancé?"

"No, thank you. Just keep me posted about the case." When Constance hung up, her hands were shaking. She wanted nothing to do with the police. Either explaining her own jealousy or exposing Richard. Her plan was to scare Richard a little, and she had gotten what she wanted. This was going too far.

She had no appetite, but a second Valium was more than welcome. She popped another pill, this time with a sip of orange juice, and sat by the fireplace with the photos of Richard and Sally. She had copies in a safe place, and those couldn't remain in her home.

With a final glance at each one of them, Constance threw the photos in the fire, which hissed as the paper cracked and broke, attacked by the merciless flames. When the hurtful images had disappeared, Constance pretended Richard's affair and that entire ordeal had never happened.

# HOUSTON

---

## FIVE MONTHS LATER

# 11

TEN DAYS BEFORE the wedding, Constance was in the presidential suite of the Hyatt Regency Hotel. Her personal assistant, Louise, had scheduled the final adjustments on the wedding gown, and for hair and makeup rehearsal to happen smoothly along the afternoon, accompanied by gourmet snacks and champagne for Constance and her bridesmaids.

Constance kept everyone waiting downstairs. She was supposed to be happy today, but all she could think about was Sally Landry.

While Richard later swore the crime happened after he left, Constance wasn't sure she believed him. Her decent side had urged her to tell the police. The selfish one reminded her that now that she knew Richard's secret, she might get more devotion from him through fear than through love.

Constance made peace with her dilemma the very day of Sally's death and since the evening they sealed their pact, she and Richard never talked about the subject. It was Constance's private investigator who kept feeding her backstage information about the case.

The last thing shown on the news was the police saying that crime rates had increased in East Boston, and gang members spent time learning the family's routines before the robberies. The Landrys were an easy target with both doctors spending ample hours at Beth Israel and Massachusetts General hospitals.

Her investigator had called that morning and told her that the mysterious caller never came forward. "As there was no reason to suspect John Landry or anyone else, a robbery seemed the most likely," he said. "Of course, if the police had known about the victim's affair, they would have investigated further. With no evidence to suspect foul play, they're about to close the case."

Playfully, Constance said, "I like the version that John Landry does it. That bitch ruined my life, and I enjoy imagining myself in his place squeezing her neck!"

The investigator laughed. He wondered why men were more logical than women about cheating. Men tended to hate their cheating partners, while women hated their rivals. Aloud, he said, "Hopefully this was truly a robbery gone wrong and your fiancé was just at the wrong place that night."

"Yes, and I'll send you a bonus for your discretion."

"No need," he said. "Don't worry, Ms. Carlton. You paid me handsomely, and what I know will never be revealed. Happy customers keep my business lucrative."

The hotel phone was ringing madly, and Constance ignored it. It was probably Louise asking her if they could come up.

*Not yet.* Constance filled a glass of champagne and barely touched it. She was fantasizing about killing Sally Landry again. She knew she lacked the self-control and cold blood required for revenge, and the best she had managed was benefiting from the aftermath of that crime.

She was a coward and that's why Sally Landry would live in her mind, forever punishing her for not getting justice for her death.

Today, the woman was definitely haunting her. Constance headed to the window, the large city below giving her perspective. "I'm smart, kind, and wealthy. I'll have a wonderful life."

"No you won't!" Sally sat on the hotel bed sipping on the champagne Constance had left. She laughed and said, "He doesn't love you."

Sally's voice still caused the same distress it did when Constance listened to it on tape. Only now it could go on for hours with no stop button to give her a break. After weeks of that drill, Constance was on the verge of a nervous breakdown.

Completely naked except for her flip flops, she paced the room, shaking her arms and taking deep breaths. She needed to get the tension out of her body, or she would have a panic attack when they zipped up the stupid gown.

"I need to talk to someone!" Constance started to call Dr. Kessler's office but hung up on the second ring. A psychiatrist would be legally obligated to inform any possible criminal activities to the police.

After a few unsuccessful trips back and forth, Constance called Victoria. "Mom, I need you here."

Louise, the bridesmaids, and the team of professionals sat in the reception area of the hotel when Victoria arrived. "Mrs. Carlton!" Louise rushed to meet her. "Can I have a word?"

Victoria did not stop, and Louise followed her to the elevator.

"My daughter is feeling ill. Please double everyone's fees and ask them to give us another hour."

Finally at her daughter's door, Victoria knocked. "Connie, I'm here."

Constance was in her robe, her face red from crying.

"Oh, darling, what happened?"

Constance looked at her mother and immediately knew the truth could not come out of her mouth. And if her mother wouldn't support her, no one would. She hugged Victoria. "My nerves are killing me. Please stick around, Mom."

The church was adorned by such an abundance of flowers the wedding seemed to take place at an enchanted garden whose greens and colorful blooms grew freely along the aisle, the marble columns, and the arches of the altar.

Constance looked regal in a hand-beaded white gown designed in Milan. Her arm in her father's, she beamed at her guests as she slowly walked toward Richard. The aisle, like Constance's veil, was a mile long and both she and Richard had time to feel every step of that decision. Constance was finally at peace. She loved Richard, and now with a solid bond, they would be happy.

Behind his frozen smile, Richard was thinking that by saying *I do* he was selling his soul to that devil in white. What had begun as a no-risk investment had surprisingly turned against him. With those compromising photos of him and Sally in Constance's safety deposit box, literally only death could tear them apart. A very unsuspicious death that should occur in a couple of years, after he had developed a splendid clientele and proved to the Carltons what a marvelous husband he was. Richard recalled his days of medical school when another weak woman had threatened his dreams. It hadn't been hard to talk Theresa Dawson into suicide. Now, more experienced, he would leave no traces.

The foreboding music of the church organ seemed to read Richard's mind, but not the minister's. The old man smiled at him and said, "Weddings always make the groom nervous. Don't worry, son. It will be over soon."

*Not as soon as I had planned.*

107

During the party, several of the Carltons' friends congratulated Richard on his upcoming clinic and promised to become his patients. Half a dozen said they would be the first to go under his knife. A constant smile on his face, Richard answered their questions and told amusing tales about his profession. Some of those people had previously chatted with him during the engagement party and would pat him on the shoulder and shake his hand as if he already belonged.

From a distance, Victoria told Timothy, "Look how everyone loves Richard. I guess some men don't come from money but pave their own way."

"I was thinking the same, and one thing is certain. He won't depend on our money for long. Let's pray he truly loves Connie."

Through his peripheral view, Richard noticed his in-laws watching him and they seemed proud. That was a marvelous sign. If he embodied the perfect son, perhaps their profitable relationship could last long after he got Constance out of the picture.

# 12

RICHARD AND CONSTANCE would live in one of the family's properties in the fancy neighborhood of Memorial. A five-bedroom modern triplex with a pool, sauna, and tennis court. Constance said they should try it for a couple of years and see if they wanted something new.

Their honeymoon would begin three days after the wedding with a trip back to Rio de Janeiro. When Richard was getting ready for them to go to the airport, Constance appeared at his dressing room and said, "I don't wanna go back to Rio. We were different people then, and I want something new."

Richard chuckled. "Kind of late to change your mind. It's all planned."

"Plans are made to be changed. I already called Louise and she's taking care of everything. We're going to Turks and Caicos."

Constance could be a child and Richard spoiled her, allegedly out of pure devotion. Despite the cards in her sleeves, he never acted like he was not in control. "As long as you're there, any place will do."

Money was really a powerful force. With a delay of mere hours, they were on a different flight, and a driver awaited them at their destination to take them to a luxurious villa overlooking the ocean.

When they arrived, Constance started dancing around the living room, then turned to Richard and pulled down the sleeves of her dress, proudly revealing her breasts.

"Want some time with these beauties?"

They made love in the largest bed Richard had ever seen and in the following days went swimming and walked hand in hand on the beach. As when they were in Brazil, Richard was very protective of Constance, never taking her out during the day without a hat or applying sunscreen on her.

"You're my guardian angel," she said, often after a kiss. "It moves me how well you take care of me." And it really did. Whenever bad memories threatened to cloud her mind, Constance tried to focus on Richard's devotion, and her insecurities tended to dissipate.

A private chef prepared their favorite dishes, and a butler brought them cocktails whenever they called for it. Richard sat outside one breezy afternoon, mojito in hand, watching the villa's infinity pool merge into the turquoise sea.

On his wedding day, envisioning years of wait

beside Constance made him feel claustrophobic. Now, surrounded by the outrageous luxuries he had always dreamed of, he thought that staying married while he grew his business shouldn't be so tough. Despite her flaws, Constance adored him, and perhaps, as she had suggested, he could forget about the leash around his neck if they were happy.

The first evening they went to a restaurant, they were helped by an attractive twenty-year-old woman with long brown hair and a captivating smile. "Good evening! Welcome to The Grove."

The waitress, who introduced herself as Jenna, was equally attentive to Constance and Richard, offering their most popular cocktails and explaining the specials on the menu.

When Jenna left to get their drinks, Constance said, "I know you prefer brunettes, but don't be disrespectful."

Richard was shocked. "Constance, you're not serious. Are you?"

"I'm dead serious and don't do it again."

"For Christ's sake, she's a kid and I barely looked at her."

"You don't need to look. I know what you're thinking."

Constance had never acted that way, and Richard looked blankly at the menu trying to figure out what to do next.

"What are you having?" she asked a moment later, and she seemed relaxed as if nothing had happened.

"Not sure yet." Initially he'd been between the mahi-mahi and a local fish he'd never tried. He intended to ask the waitress what she recommended, but after Constance's lecture, he took no chances. When Jenna returned, Richard kept his eyes on the menu while she took Constance's order and ordered the wahoo.

The waitress seemed amused. "Have you tried this fish before, sir?"

"No."

Jenna laughed. "Well done! I love adventurous clients. I'll replace it if you don't like it."

Before Richard could utter a word, Constance said, "No worries, dear, my husband loves adventures. Now if we can have some privacy."

"Of course, ma'am."

"And I'd like to have another server."

Richard couldn't tell how good the wahoo fish or anything else on his plate was. After Constance's scene, everything tasted like beach sand. The woman was acting crazy. What the fuck would he do now?

The rest of that evening was uneventful, and Richard chose not to confront Constance about her behavior, at least while they were abroad.

More than once in the span of the next few days, he caught her in bikinis studying her body in front of the mirror. One morning, she went shopping and returned with a blue summer dress almost identical to the waitress's. Richard knew that was a bad sign. Constance had enough complexes without comparing herself to other women. He didn't mention anything.

Constance put on her new acquisition, and he wasn't sure what would cause more trouble, complimenting her or not. He chose his words carefully—"Pretty as usual!"—and offered his arm. "Let's go?"

They had lunch in the village and returned to enjoy the pool. While Richard was inside on the phone with the contractor working on his clinic, Constance fell asleep on a stretcher and didn't notice that the umbrella didn't fully cover her. Richard was inside for nearly an hour. When he was finished, he prepared two margaritas and headed outside.

Constance was in the pool wailing like a child who had lost her mother.

Richard left the drinks at a table and jumped in. As he approached her, he saw red patches on her face and body and thought of allergies. "Can you breathe?"

"I'm burned," she whispered. "You left me out to burn."

"What?"

"Look at me!" she screamed, and then her voice dropped to a whisper again. "You love the beach, and I did it for you. Now I look like a monster."

"I thought you loved the beach too."

"I hate it! Always did."

Richard took a deep breath. "And you don't look like a monster. Your skin is just irritated." He examined her left arm, which seemed the reddest, and said, "You'll be fine in a day or two." He found a cream in his first aid kit to calm Constance's skin and a few hours later, she had no discomfort.

That evening, after she took a cool bath, Richard reapplied the cream and Constance said, "Sorry I said this was your fault. I was feeling terrible."

"It's okay, honey. Let's put it in the past."

"Yeah. All bad things should stay in the past."

Richard pretended not to understand her implication. It had been naive to think he'd be able to lower his guard in this marriage. Constance was the enemy. She always would be.

As promised, two days later, Constance's skin looked slightly tanned with no signs of the red patches. She showed up naked while Richard was in the den reading. "I feel pretty again! Still love your bride?"

Richard summoned all his power to get an erection. He brought Constance to the couch and penetrated her gently as usual, but he was angry. As not to hit her in the face, like he wanted, Richard fucked her hard. Hard as he fucked the women he was really attracted to.

He was waiting for Constance to stop him, to call him a brute. Instead, she said, "Harder, baby!"

Richard thought of Sally, hands on his butt, guiding him deeper and deeper inside her.

"Harder!" Constance screamed, and Richard climaxed with a loud groan.

For the first time since they'd started dating, Constance seemed insatiable.

"We belong to each other now," she said, looking at her wedding ring. "Are you happy, my love?"

"Very happy. And I'll be happier if you trust me."

"Can I do that now that you're my husband?"

"You have my word."

Constance had always been insecure about her body. Richard knew it had been hard on her that he'd cheated. Even harder that it happened *after* her breast surgery. Maybe if he demonstrated more desire, paid her more compliments, she would gradually feel safer.

Again, he was wrong.

They spent the following two days in bed, getting out only for eating and showering, and suddenly Constance said, "When you fuck me like that, I know you're thinking of her. Will she ever leave us?"

From there, no matter what he did, the honeymoon was over.

# 13

RICHARD WAS RELIEVED to return to Houston and start hiring doctors and staff for his clinic. They would open in a few months, and he wanted to put all his energy there. Since Constance's comments about Sally in bed and her excessive jealously in their final days in Turks and Caicos, he had tried to reason with her.

"Darling, you found out about Sally months ago. You said you still wanted to marry me. What's triggering this?"

Constance stayed quiet. Eyes blank as if she were sedated.

"Our marriage won't work if you don't let this go," he continued.

Finally, she responded, "I can't let it go if you think about her in bed and see her in every woman!"

"I think you should adjust your anxiety medication.

Something is off since the wedding and it's nothing I'm doing."

Sometimes Constance listened to him and calmed down. Sometimes she blamed him for ruining their lives and gave him the cold treatment for a few days. Their first month of marriage was a roller coaster.

Richard's main concern was Constance's loose tongue. She'd been talking a lot about Sally recently, and he feared she would end up, accidentally or not, sharing their secrets. When Constance invited her parents for dinner, Richard was on high alert.

The dinner invitation was for seven thirty at their new home, and the Carltons were punctual. Richard greeted them at the door. "Welcome! Constance is still getting ready. She asked her hairdresser to come over."

Richard was wearing a light blue jacket that brought up his tan, and Victoria said, "You look handsome, my dear. I bet you two had a wonderful time in the islands."

"We definitely did! I'll let my wife tell you more."

"Your wife," Victoria said and laughed. "I love how the word rolls off your tongue."

Richard smiled. "It's been nice getting used to it." They moved into the vast living room and Richard said, "Please have a seat. What would you like to drink?"

Dinner was supposed to be informal, but as they small talked about Timothy's business, Constance showed up at the top of the staircase wearing a tight white gown. Her blond hair had been dyed black and cut at ear length.

Richard almost dropped his glass. At a distance, she looked like Sally Landry.

The Carltons glanced at Richard, and by the expression on his face, they realized that the look was a novelty for him as well.

Victoria tried to save the day. "Darling! You look fabulous!"

Constance smiled and came down the stairs, combing her hair with her fingers. "Thank you, Mom! A new life deserves a makeover." She looked at Richard. "Don't you think, honey?"

He managed a smiled. "Absolutely. You look stunning."

"What do you think, Dad? Am I pretty enough now?"

Timothy looked at his daughter with visible discomfort and wondered when exactly she had started to lose her marbles. "You look marvelous, sweetheart."

Victoria wouldn't allow the air to get any heavier. She hooked Constance's arm with hers and said, "I'm starving! Let's head to the table."

Richard would sit at the head of the table. Before doing so, he pulled a chair for Victoria on his left and one for Constance on his right. Timothy sat beside Victoria and went back to safe subjects. "Richard, how's it going with the clinic?"

"All on time to open after Labor Day. The contractor said the building is new and needed very little structural work before starting the renovation."

"Richard has wonderful taste," Constance said,

proud as usual. "The colors, the lighting. The place looks more like a hotel than a clinic."

Richard hoped Constance's mood stayed colorful and light as well. "Thank you, sweetheart. I must have been inspired by your wonderful taste decorating this home."

Victoria nodded. "That was an amazing job, Connie! This house had great bones but no personality. Looks wonderful now."

"I feel wonderful!" Constance grabbed Richard's hand. "And very loved. Richard is a dream husband."

Richard kissed her hand. "I'm trying to be."

She held his gaze for a moment as if she wanted to believe him, then turned back to her parents and shrieked. "Guess what I'll be doing here in Houston?"

"I thought you would join the committee of the Museum of Fine Arts," Timothy said.

"Nah, I need a break from the arts. Remember when I was younger how much fun I had volunteering for wildlife protection?"

Timothy remembered her making a speech about the cruelties of African safaris at one of their parties, making two of his close friends leave. "I remember. The group protected elephants' rights?"

"Exactly. I want to get involved with that kind of stuff again. Don't you think we're all too self-centered?" Without waiting for anyone's response, she said, "In Turks and Caicos I was looking at the ocean and started thinking of the garbage people throw there, the dying sea life. I've decided to become more involved with animals and the environment."

Constance monopolized the conversation while the staff served the appetizers and main courses, and everyone played along, nodding, smiling, and agreeing with whatever stupidity she uttered as if she were a queen.

Richard hoped that saving the dolphins would keep the bitch busy. What he enjoyed the most that evening was her parents' fake expressions trying to mask their concern. Constance had no idea what a favor her growing eccentricities were doing for his cause. The crazier she looked and acted, the easier it would be for everyone to believe that her mind was frail and she could do something stupid.

# 14

RICHARD HAD DEEPLY studied the plastic surgery market in Houston and decided that their strongest offers would be face rejuvenation, nose jobs, liposuction, and breast augmentation. To start, he hired an administrator to run the clinic and put together the operational staff. He personally selected the nurses and three of his Harvard colleagues. Two plastic surgeons, who would each specialize in one type of procedure, and an anesthesiologist. Like Richard, the other doctors were in their mid-thirties and were excited to grow a practice together, quite aware that Richard had the money and would officially be the boss.

Richard had always been fascinated by the face, and after learning Dr. Pitanguy's subtle magic, that became his specialty. He would handle everything from the

neck up. Dr. Clark Moore would be the breast special-
ist, and Dr. Robert Stein would focus on liposuction.

When it came to medical procedures, word of
mouth was the best form of advertising, and yet, since
Richard had the money to appear in full-page ads, he
attacked from both fronts. New trends were shaping up
that year, and penile augmentation and butt implants
would be among the next items in the institute's PR
plan. Reconstructive surgery would be taken case by
case, not advertised. Richard wanted The Wilken Institute of Plastic Surgery to be known as a place of beauty
and youth.

Constance had started dressing like a twenty-year-
old and going out with new friends from the Wildlife
Conservancy projects. Victoria called her every day.
"What are you trying to accomplish, Connie?"

"Relax, Mom. I'm not bothering Richard or any of
you. I just hadn't realized how much time I wasted
buried in my complexes. I feel so alive!"

One day, Constance appeared at the Institute unan-
nounced and told Richard, "I want liposuction. My ass
and thighs are enormous!"

Constance was lifting weights and trying a different
diet every day. She had dropped twenty pounds. Mercifully, her hair was back to its natural sandy blond.

Richard did not discuss. "If you want to stick around
after his consultations, Stein will see you."

"Thanks."

She remained sitting across from Richard's desk,
and in her short dress and boots, chewing bubble gum

as she looked outside the window, she incarnated a rebellious teenager. After a moment, Constance looked at Richard, who, now used to her new persona, seemed unfazed reading a medical paper and making notes.

"Do you think I need liposuction?" she asked.

"No."

She got up. "It's because you haven't seen me naked for weeks." In a fluid movement, Constance lifted her dress above her head. In her bra and panties, she pinched the tiny amount of fat on her abdomen. She had lost over fifteen pounds in the past couple of months. "See? I'm becoming a fat cow like when we dated." She proceeded to pinch the skin on her ass and thighs and said, "Do you agree now?"

"I think you look good, but the decision is yours and your doctor's." He got up and picked a gown in the closet. "Wear this. I'll ask Stein to see you here."

Richard left and Constance smiled, proud of herself.

That was the type of woman Richard liked. Skinny and independent. That's why she had been on a diet and pretended not to care about his opinions. She had even changed her hair color back to her natural blond, knowing he preferred brunettes. That would cause a bigger impact later when she put her amazing look together. As a plastic surgeon, Richard would admire someone who built their best selves block by block.

By their first anniversary, Constance looked like a different woman. She even looked taller than her five foot eight, weighing only 126 pounds. Like her breasts, her lips, butt, and calves were pools of silicone, and every inch of her body had endured liposculpture, a procedure that transferred fat excessive in one area of the body to another that could benefit from a natural filler. The effect was incredible.

The scalpel hadn't yet touched Constance's face. The same couldn't be stated about fillers and Botox. Her fair skin, so intolerant to the sun, was now three shades darker by artificial tanning, and with her latest long brown mane, she was finally a proud brunette.

# HOUSTON

---

## TWO YEARS LATER

# 15

*Brain* was what he called himself whenever he addressed his plan. Richard was a genius and had such a complex personality that any of his enemies should have a powerful pseudonym to even consider outsmarting him. Over the years, watching and waiting, *Brain* he became.

Richard had no idea what Brain thought or felt about him. Not when Brain admired him or when, among other white coats, Brain had almost stabbed him in the chest.

How blissful that destiny had held Brain's hand years ago. Planning always outshined improvisation, and wearing a mask was a wiser weapon. One that allowed you to stay close to your target while remaining invisible.

It was January of 1989. Watching George H.W. Bush's presidential inauguration on TV, Richard had his own winnings to celebrate. Twenty-seven months since The Wilken Institute of Plastic Surgery had opened its doors, Richard's career had exceeded his expectations.

Ten plastic surgeons worked for him doing every cosmetic procedure on the menu, and Richard remained the sole king of facelifts. That was his baby. The differentiator that put him on the cover of *People* magazine and got him interviews on *Good Morning America* and *Larry King.*

Recently nicknamed "Dr. Youth," Richard became known as the American master of rejuvenating the face with a natural look. He was booked for the entire next year, and his waiting list was already in the hundreds. Even Dr. Ivo Pitanguy called to congratulate him: "I'm proud of you, Richard. Keep up the great work!"

He intended to. Only now, he could no longer do it under Constance's shadow. Despite his wife's mood swings and fits of jealously, which became part of their routine, she had kept her promises, the good ones and the bad.

Walter Lehman, a lawyer and financial expert, was the actual gatekeeper of the Carltons' fortune, both Constance's and her parents. As promised when he signed his prenup and a dozen other agreements, Richard received his clinic and the money he needed to make it bloom.

Lehman was instructed, however, to not provide a dime to Richard's personal needs without Constance's approval. That was her constant reminder that he belonged to her and leaving his golden cage would only put him behind other bars. Richard had accounts with fancy tailors and stores for clothes and accessories and a credit card for his other expenses. Monthly, he received a humiliating nominal fee of one thousand dollars in his bank account and a call from Lehman to justify any non-obvious items in stores or on credit card statements.

Richard had built his life around the goal of becoming rich, and now that he was, on his own merits, the circumstances were laughable. He was making hundreds of thousands and living like a boy, begging daddy to increase his allowance. Lucky for him, he was a patient boy.

Alone in his home studio, Richard filled a glass of champagne and raised it to the TV where Bush was making his oath. "To a new man in power!"

Richard emptied his glass without a pause and refilled it. He headed to the window and contemplated their enormous property. That side of their new mansion in River Oaks faced the pool and the green grass. Richard tried to stay away from his bedroom window, which was right above the bizarre garden Constance had designed. Initially it would be like a mini Versailles, with elegant plants and mazes. Halfway through the project, Constance decided to turn it into a cross between a tropical forest and the Hanging Gardens of Babylon. A horrendous canvas depicting his wife's mental health.

After what seemed an eternity, Richard had gained his fame and the Carltons' respect for being a devoted husband.

It was time for Constance to die.

Richard's in-laws would come for lunch today, along with a friend of Constance's from the Wildlife Conservancy and her husband. Richard was in no mood to chat with Timothy about politics or with the other losers about the importance of recycling. Richard looked at his watch. He had one hour of peace before showtime.

Downstairs, Constance sat at the veranda beside George, her adopted chimpanzee. George was five and had the discipline of a child that age. When Richard found them, George was walking on the table their staff had set up for lunch licking a spoon and messing with the flower arrangements.

"Get out of there!" Richard screamed.

Like a spoiled child, George remained in place and glanced at Constance as if waiting for her to defend him.

"Get out now!" Richard folded a newspaper and hit the table near George. The loud bang made him shriek and jump out, then run outside.

*Disgusting creature.*

"What have you done to him?" Constance was walking toward Richard carrying George, whose arms were wrapped around her neck.

"Exactly what the vet told us to do when he misbehaves."

Constance smoothed George's face as if he were a child. "Don't worry. Mom's not gonna let him hurt you."

It required superhuman efforts for Richard not to roll his eyes. "The guests must be arriving. Please give me some bullet points for conversation with the Reynolds."

She made a dismissive gesture with her hand. "No need to pretend, if you don't care for our cause."

"I care for the environment, but every day you guys are saving a different animal. I can't keep up."

"You see, George? He hates animals."

"I don't hate animals. I hate this bullshit! And can you stop talking to the monkey when I'm talking to you?"

Constance smiled, and when Richard turned around, her parents were behind him.

Richard closed his eyes, regretting the altercation. At that point, the three of them were used to overlooking Constance's growing eccentricities. The radical changes in her appearance, a trip to Costa Rica as a volunteer in a wildlife shelter, then wanting a new home, the garden, and most recently, adopting a chimpanzee. What was unusual for Timothy and Victoria was seeing Richard out of control. In two and a half years of marriage, he had been a patient, devoted husband, and the media attention he received for being such a successful doctor made the Carltons proud.

Richard tried to make a joke. "Sorry, George is competitive. Sometimes it's like sharing my wife with another man!"

Timothy patted his back. "I couldn't put up with a cat. Civilized people have dogs."

Richard lowered his voice. "Don't tell your daughter, but I'm with you."

The two walked away to talk about business while Constance and Victoria caught up on the past hour's gossip. The two spoke on the phone all day.

Patricia and Larry Reynolds arrived, and the three couples enjoyed mimosas and hors d'oeuvres by the monstrous garden everyone pretended to find interesting.

Patricia let out a sigh. "These purple palm trees are gorgeous, Connie. Where do they come from again?"

"My friends in Costa Rica got them for me. And the shrono tree over there is a type of swamp vegetation; that's why we had to add a lake to the project."

At the table, since everybody was a Republican, the conversation started with the highlights of Bush's campaign and today's inauguration, then tragically for Richard and Constance's parents, returned to the wildlife topic.

Staring at the Reynolds, Richard had the same visceral reaction he had when he looked at Constance. *Brainless motherfuckers. You'd be dead without a family fund.*

Richard was half spacing out when Constance stood up. "My dearest ones, I invited you here because I have an important announcement. I'm pregnant."

# 16

IT HAD NEVER been harder for Richard to get his act together. He couldn't even pretend he'd already heard the news. He just tried to turn his petrified facial expression into something that resembled a positive surprise. Then he smiled, hugged Constance, and froze his thoughts for later. As he accepted hugs and congratulations from everybody, he wished it wouldn't be terribly suspicious if Constance drowned in the bathtub that night.

When the door finally closed behind the last guest, Richard turned to Constance. "How could you keep this from me?"

"I wanted to make it a surprise."

"I thought you were on the pill."

"I was, but it was making me fat and I stopped."

"Without telling me?"

"You've been so busy. We have sex, what, once a week?"

"Apparently enough to get you pregnant."

"And isn't that wonderful?"

"Do I look like I find it wonderful?"

"You're in shock like all men when they get the news."

"I don't think this is a good idea. We're not ready to be parents."

"Why not? Your work is successful, my work is successful, of course we're ready!"

Richard didn't know what was more absurd—Constance comparing his career to her charity, or thinking they had a solid enough structure to have a child. "I don't want to be a father, and this wasn't an accident. You can't force this on me."

"Do you want me to have an abortion?"

"That's the only thing to do."

Constance looked down. When she spoke, her voice was almost timid. "You never loved me, did you?"

"Of course I love you, but having this baby is a bad decision."

She was mute for a moment, then asked, "Would you have broken up our engagement if Sally Landry was pregnant?"

"For Christ's sake, woman! How many times do I have to tell you that Sally and I were just fucking? No one was in love!"

"Good to know, because my investigator told me

that she was, and the husband was devastated. But it could have been yours, right?"

Richard was speechless and blanching for just long enough, then Constance broke out laughing. "Gotcha! She wasn't pregnant. I just wanted to see your face!"

"You're sick! That's not funny."

"Nothing is funny anymore. That's why, like it or not, we're having this baby."

"I don't think that's the way things work."

Connie shrugged. "That's the way it's gonna be."

"Fine. I need some fresh air tonight. I'll skip dinner."

"Don't do anything silly."

"I just need silence and a goddamn drink!"

After so long of behaving as a respectful husband, Richard perceived the dark, crowded bar of the St. Regis as a scene from a film he had watched decades ago. Unlike his happy days in Boston, he wasn't there to network, flirt, or even drink much. He wanted to sit alone, order a martini, and feel like a man who hadn't spent the past few years under his wife's thumb. Oblivious to the loud music and chatting, Richard stared at the olive submersed in his drink like he was meditating.

Thinking of his plans always brought him the resolve to endure the tough gap separating planning and achieving. He was planning to get rid of Constance by manipulating her psychiatric meds. Now, pregnant, her doctor would decrease the dosages and he might not get the results he needed. He began to break down the plan in small steps to see how far he could go.

"Richard Wilken."

The intrusive voice belonged to a face Richard remembered but couldn't place.

Noticing his blank expression, the man said, "Peter Brown. We were contemporaries at Harvard."

*Dr. Nobody.* The resident from anesthesia who had broken the news to him about Sally's murder. Richard smiled. "I apologize, Peter, I'm terrible with names!"

"No worries, we were never close. I thought it must be you because I saw you on TV and knew you were living here. What an accomplishment, huh?"

"What can I say? I love what I do."

All the bar seats were taken, and Richard said, "Do you wanna try to get a table?"

"Next time. I'm leaving."

"Visiting?"

"No. I've been hired by Mercy Hospital."

"Congratulations! So I'll be seeing you again."

Richard offered his hand and Peter shook it. *You definitely will.*

To Richard's despair, Constance was awake when he returned.

"Can we talk more now that you're relaxed?" she asked.

"If you came to your senses."

"I can't have an abortion, Richard. I'm three months along."

"What? You told everybody you just got the news!"

"I lied. I knew you'd suggest an abortion, and now you know it's too late for it."

Richard scoffed. "As usual, you had a plan to trap me."

"You and your obsession with trapping." Constance imitated his voice. "You trapped me into waving my money. You trapped me into having a baby."

Richard did not join her laughing, and Constance said, "I'm not manipulating you. I think you make bad decisions about relationships, and if I guide you a bit, things work better."

"Guide me? Since our honeymoon, you've been acting crazy and pushing me around. I wonder if you realize what a turn-off that is. Why would I want a child to share our misery?"

Constance looked Richard in the eye. "You're right. I've been angry and trying to hurt you for what you did in Boston, but this baby will save us. I promise I'll be myself again and be good to both of you."

*No you won't. I'll need to get you out of my way.* Richard pretended to deliberate so Constance wouldn't find it too easy to convince him. After a moment staring at his hands, he looked up at her. "Okay, let's try this."

"Really?"

"Really."

Constance hugged Richard, her face glowing. "You won't regret this, darling! Would you come to the doctor with me this week?"

A nurse measured Constance's vitals and weight, and a moment later, Dr. Claire Simmons entered the room.

"This is my husband," Constance said.

The doctor shook Richard's hand and said in a thick Texan accent, "A pleasure to meet you, Mr. Wilken."

"Dr. Wilken."

"Oh yes, your wife mentioned you were a plastic surgeon. The Wilken Institute, right?"

The two made small talk for a few minutes and Dr. Simmons told Constance, "You are very lucky your husband is a doctor. A pregnancy can be a simple or a complex experience, and having another trained pair of eyes following the process is a privilege."

"Do you see any specific concerns we should be attentive to?" Richard asked.

"Only Constance's anxiety medications. She told me sometimes she self-medicates, increasing or decreasing the dosages according to how she feels, and I told her that will be harmful to the baby. I spoke to her psychiatrist, and we agreed to the minimal doses to keep Constance comfortable, and she promised to stick to them."

"I will, Doctor. The baby is more important than anything."

While Dr. Simmons seemed satisfied, Richard didn't believe Constance would keep that promise. Actually, he was counting on it.

Dr. Simmons selected four bottles from a cabinet behind her. "And these are vitamins you'll take twice every day to help you and the baby."

The doctor looked at Richard. "Constance said she tends to forget the exact time of her medications. Please get someone to take care of it."

Richard studied the translucent bottles and was happy the vitamins came in capsules instead of solid pills. He could open them without causing any suspicion and replace their contents. He could cause a miscarriage in a week, and later, combining Constance's sadness with the psychiatric drugs he had in mind, she would become so depressed that, as in her adolescence, a mean comment could push her to end her life. No one would suspect him. Constance self-medicated, bought prescription drugs on the black market, and had tried suicide before.

"All right," said Dr. Simmons, bringing him back. "Now the best part. Let's see the baby."

Richard had read that a new generation of ultrasound equipment was being used by ob-gyns to monitor the fetus, look for malformations, and discover the sex of the baby. He hadn't seen it in action, though, and hesitated. Why see a baby he was trying to kill? "I'm not sure I wanna know the sex," he said.

Constance shook his arm. "Don't be silly, honey! It's a miracle they now have this technology. I've been excited about it for weeks!"

Dr. Simmons said, "I can show you the fetus without telling you the sex."

She waited and finally Richard nodded.

The image of the baby was already fascinating. The first ultrasound image of a fetus Richard had seen out of a medical magazine. He initially stared at it like a novelty in medical class. A foreign subject detached from his reality.

When the doctor turned on the speaker, the baby's heartbeat took over the room. The room and something else Richard didn't know existed. His throat became too tight for the air to pass. His well-trained heart ignored his commands.

The screen was no longer displaying a mere image. He was looking at a person with hands and eyes, staring at him. That was his child, who telepathically seemed to know his plan. The baby moved as the overpowering heartbeat continued, and Richard felt a tear stain his cheek.

Dr. Simmons grinned. "That's very impactful, Doctor Wilken. Especially when it's your kid."

The baby lost Constance's interest. Richard was crying out of the emotion of having their child, and that was prettier than anything. "Darling," she said, moved too.

Richard smiled. "That was not very manly."

"That was perfectly fine," said the doctor. "Do you want to know the sex?"

"Yes, please." Richard said.

"Congratulations! It's a boy."

# 17

BRAIN'S APARTMENT APPEARED to always be strikingly hot, no matter how low the number on the thermostat. Maybe because he was burning inside with expectation. Or because no matter how long he lived there, he would never adjust to the southern weather. Only a very serious mission could have brought him to scorching Texas.

He sat at the table and opened a folder. Long ago, he had foreseen that Richard would appear on those magazine covers and in newspaper articles clipped there. What he couldn't have imagined was Richard's being a father.

The man was short of a heart or owned one just capable of self-love. The article in today's paper seemed surreal. Richard standing by the pool of his mansion, his arms around the growing belly of that disgusting bitch. Constance Carlton.

Even saying her name aloud caused him visceral hatred. Looking at her happily enjoying life with Richard was beyond his tolerance level.

There would be no clipping of that article.

Brain tore the page out, lit a match against Constance's face, and watched it burn.

Richard had bought an ultrasound machine for the clinic so he would be able to monitor the baby's development during the entire pregnancy.

"Isn't that bad for the baby to do it too often?" Constance asked.

"By no means. It's not like X-ray. It's sound waves that form images. And it's important to know if a fetus is properly growing inside the womb. With this, I can measure his size from head to abdomen and check if it meets the growth chart."

"I thought Dr. Simmons was doing that."

"Well, it doesn't hurt to do it again."

Richard spilled gel on Constance's belly and started moving the ultrasound wand back and forward, and more than studying the fetus, he seemed to be caressing his son.

Constance put her hand on Richard's. "It's wonderful to see you so excited about becoming a father. I told you this baby would bring us closer."

Richard didn't feel any closer to Constance. He had never loved her and recently had no respect for her.

She was the vessel carrying a precious diamond. The moment the cargo arrived at its destination, she would again become disposable. Richard planned to allow her only enough time to breastfeed his son and attend to the infant's initial needs before motherhood proved to be too much for her and she parted this world.

Richard was secretly learning the triggers of postpartum depression, and now, for the baby's sake, he would take even greater risks, like creating an accident if Constance didn't succumb to the drugs he planned to feed her. Bad mothers were a poison he'd been luckily deprived of. He would do anything so his son wouldn't suffer any influence of that mental case.

Richard got a driver to take Constance home safely and went back to his office, where he reevaluated the Institute's six-month business plan.

On his current team, there were three doctors doing breast surgery, three doing liposuction, two doing abdominal work, one doing buttock and calf implants, one doing penile augmentation and vaginal rejuvenation, and only him handling everything facial. Nose jobs, eyelids, cheek implants, and facelifts kept him busy, with up to five surgeries a day. So far, nothing could have made him happier. He was doing what he loved and had little time to think about his marriage or its limitations until he could reclaim his freedom.

With the baby and later implementing his plan to become a widower, Richard could no longer monopolize his specialty. He would need two more doctors to help him with the facial work or the Institute would lose serious money while he was away. He would start recruiting and would spend the next five months until the baby's birth training and supervising his replacements.

Richard picked up the phone. "Samantha, can you come to my office, please?"

Samantha Reeves was the administrator of the clinic. With a staff of fifteen, she ran everything from scheduling surgeries to processing payments, getting supplies, and paying the salaries of everyone under that roof.

Samantha made her way from her office on the ground level to Richard's on the second floor performing her usual inspection of the plant. If the flower arrangements were fresh, if the cleaning team hadn't left any spots on the marble and windows. If the receptionists' appearances obeyed their checklist. It was a temple of beauty guarded by a woman allergic to vanity.

Samantha laughed inside when she thought about it. Had the famous Dr. Wilken seen her on her days off, with no makeup, messy hair, and wearing clothes twice her size, she wouldn't have gotten that job. Thirty-seven-year-old Sam, as she preferred to be called, had grown up with an excessively vain mother and despised all sorts of body cult. Ironically, it was a plastic surgery clinic that offered her the best salary and benefits in the market, and she'd been with them from the beginning.

Sam walked into the ladies' room and stared at her alter ego in the mirror. There, her makeup impeccable, blond hair in an updo, wearing expensive suits and Chanel shoes, she did look the part.

A minute later, her manicured hand knocked at Richard's door, and after a

"Come in," she entered his office.

Richard intrigued Sam. Like most women there, she'd noticed his athletic body and elegant style. She found Richard attractive, and yet there seemed to be something amiss. He was polite, with a warmth that animated his smile without reflecting in his eyes.

Everyone wanted to learn from Richard Wilken, gain his compliments, attend his parties. Sam hoped to discover who he was behind his shining armor. "Do you already have anyone in mind, Dr. Wilken?"

"Not yet. I'd like you to call my connections and see if they recommend anyone fresh out of specialization. I want a young doctor I can train."

"I'll do it right away. Anything else?" Sam knew Richard didn't like to waste time, and when she finished her sentence she was already by the door.

"I'd like you to buy me some books about baby care." He smiled. "We'll have nannies, but you never know."

"Of course." Sam took notes and left. She considered herself skillful with people. Even if she hated them, she managed to pull off what seemed an honest smile, and she had the rare capacity of remaining polite and firm while dealing with temperamental personalities. She took the elevator to the third floor, where she personally handled the most demanding and complicated patients. The neurotic, delusional types who had unreasonable requests and expectations, and the celebrities and politicians who wanted full secrecy during their stay.

In fast pace, Sam headed to the fourth floor to check on more VIP accommodations for the following day, and then back to her office, which buzzed with multiple voices talking on the phone.

Sam looked at her notes and had just sat down to take care of Richard's requests when her secretary said, "Mrs. Wilken left a message for you."

Samantha sighed. She could handle the daily ups and downs in the Institute and liked almost everyone working there. Her greatest challenge was dealing with Constance. She absolutely loathed the woman and felt like she lost two years of life every time Constance asked her to resolve an issue. It was either something complicated, unethical, or virtually impossible that Constance wanted *right now*. Last time was obtaining the permit to own a goddamned monkey!

When she was hired, Samantha hoped Constance was just the boss's wife and, in time, that she'd be able to avoid those situations. What time showed her, however, was that if Richard was the brain of the Institute, Constance was the bank, and there was no escaping her. With her degree in finance, Sam joked about her unpleasant quasi-boss using math jargon. *Happily, Constance is not a constant.* She would die if she had to be face-to-face with that woman on a daily basis.

When Samantha Reeves left, Richard called Drs. Robert Stein and Clark Moore, the two surgeons who started the Institute with him. Moore was now the head of breast surgery and Stein the head of liposuction.

"Finally, you're giving yourself a break!" Moore said.

Stein nodded. "No guilt, Richard. You work hard. Take some time to enjoy your child."

"Thank you, guys. I'll be away only a couple of weeks and then decrease my number of surgeries. I'll hold a formal meeting to tell everybody but wanted you both to help me keep an eye on the newcomers. We know how we like things around here."

While Moore's face was bright and his mouth was promising they would take care of everything, his mind was screaming, *If you only knew my real plan!*

# 18

THE INTERVIEWS WITH young plastic surgeons from Harvard, Columbia, Yale, and Cornell started the following week. While Richard was excited, he wasn't impulsive about anything. Even if he loved a candidate, he simply put their name on a second list, and those finalists would go through a series of practical situations involving examining patients and assisting Richard in the operating room.

Richard remembered his days in Brazil and how quick to identify true talents Dr. Pitanguy was. He hoped he had absorbed that skill, along with the others.

On Wednesday, when he arrived home, the Carltons were there for their traditional weekly dinner. They were sitting by the pool with Constance and George on her lap. When Richard approached the group, the chimpanzee hissed.

Timothy chuckled. "The little fellow thinks he's the alpha here!"

"No," Richard said. "He knows who's the boss. He just doesn't like me."

Constance kissed George's face. "He is so lovely. Look, he's on a natural diet with me. We eat the same vegetables and fruit."

Victoria seemed worried. "Honey, what are you doing with George when the baby arrives?"

Richard responded for Constance. "I told her we'll need to get rid of him.

Apes can be aggressive, especially with children."

"Oh, look at this face," Constance baby talked. "He couldn't hurt a fly."

George seemed to understand the conversation and appeared to be sad, eyes down, completely serene.

"We're taking no chances," Richard said, and Constance shot back, now in normal voice. "We're not giving George away, either!"

Normally Richard would have continued the argument. With his in-laws there, he simply got up. "Anyone want another drink?"

When he returned with a refill for Timothy, Victoria said, "I'd like to ask you something, Richard."

"Of course."

"I met this delightful young man at our charity event, and he's a plastic surgeon from Cornell. Constance told me you're hiring, and I gave him your number."

Richard hated when anyone intruded in his business, especially family. "Thank you, Victoria. I'll be glad to speak to him."

When Tyler MacLaine shook your hand, he did it with the eyes and warmth of an old friend. "Thank you for seeing me, Dr. Wilken. This is an enormous privilege."

"Victoria said wonders about you, and my mother-in-law is not easy to impress."

Tyler smiled. "Mr. and Mrs. Carlton are incredible. I appreciate what they've done."

"Well, Tyler, most of the other candidates flew here to interview for the positions I'm offering. What brought you to Houston?"

"Same thing. I heard you were hiring, called here and sent my resume to a Samantha Reeves. But the chance of working with a surgeon of your caliber isn't something one just applies for and waits by the phone to hear about. When I learned of the charity event your mother-in-law was organizing, I bought myself a ticket and flew here. I introduced myself and point blank asked her for an introduction."

Richard smiled without noticing. He would have done the same thing. "Well done. I appreciate your determination, and your resumé is pretty impressive. I'm happy you're here. Now tell me more about your experience."

After days of discussing case studies and watching the final candidates in the operating room, Richard chose Drs. Mark Jones and Tyler MacLaine as his apprentices.

Mark Jones had graduated from Columbia and already had a job in a prestigious clinic in New York. He had been a fan of Richard's work since the Institute had opened and was happy to move to Texas to work with him.

Based on their experience, Richard intended to train both new doctors to perform nose jobs and have Jones focus on facial implants, Tyler on eyelids and facelifts.

A week after the duo was hired, a woman was having surgery to correct a previous facelift. She had a very noticeable shift in her hairline after the procedure. "What would you do, Tyler?" Richard asked.

Tyler's hands examined the woman's scalp. "She has considerable areas of hair loss around the scars. We could fix the hairline, but new hair might not grow back to cover the scars."

"So what do we do?"

"Surgically nothing. We alert the patient that for a perfect look we may need to combine our efforts with hair implants after she heals."

Tyler wasn't exaggerating when he said he'd been studying Richard's methods. He seemed to have read every article about Richard and every medical paper the man had ever published.

"You're the boss's favorite," Jones told Tyler one evening they went out for drinks. "I'm not sure I'm impressing him as much."

"I doubt that. Wilken isn't the type who allows you to stick around if you're average. I think he seems more excited when we work together simply because facelifts are his thing."

Jones took a sip of his beer. "I think I'm paranoid for other reasons."

"Please enlighten me."

"Can you keep it between us?"

"Of course."

"I'm gay, but with this AIDS shit, I'm afraid that if I come out, I won't stay in the job." He lowered his voice. "Won't even get a seat in a decent bar."

"Well, you're not the obvious type. I wouldn't know if you hadn't told me."

"Do you mind?"

"Morally, no, but I understand the threat of a mortal virus. I'd keep a low profile. People are ignorant. You don't want patients to be afraid of you."

After that conversation, Tyler never hung out with Jones outside the clinic.

Richard didn't love the idea of mixing business with personal life. He was comfortable kissing the asses of important people who could become clients and catapult him to fame and success. Throwing a party at his home for the Institute's staff was not an idea that would occur to him naturally.

Dr. Stein had come with the plan. "Richard, we'll need our staff to be their best when you're not here watching their every move."

"Samantha handles them pretty well."

"I know, but even she gets stiff when you're around."

"What are you talking about?"

"Since Harvard, you're nice to everyone, but kind of... " Stein looked for the word. "Inaccessible?"

Richard just looked at him and Stein laughed. "Trust

me, my friend, a party at your place will make the staff feel like we're a big family."

Richard thought about it. Stein was right. When he was at the Institute every day, being polite did the trick. Being away, he would need more loyalty. More eyes wanting to report back to him if something went wrong.

"Okay. Let's do it."

"Families too?"

"Not this time. I don't want anyone distracted by their children and spouses."

"That's the spirit!"

Jones enjoyed watching Richard perform surgery. There was no doubt the man was a genius, but his boss had a confidence about everything he said and did that stirred old memories and feelings. Was it possible that all strong, intelligent men were straight? How many men had he dated hoping to find a perfect match?

Richard raised his eyes from the incision and Jones felt a jolt, like his private thoughts had been highjacked. "This patient is sixty-five, and her cheeks are very flaccid. What types of implants would you recommend?"

Jones was back on firm terrain when he could rely on his brain. "Her face is sunken here and here." He indicated the spots. "I recommend submalar implants placed mid-face, below the cheekbones, to add fullness without overstretching the skin."

Richard nodded, and even though he was wearing a mask, Jones could see he was smiling. "Excellent!

I feel confident with you and Tyler replacing me. You're ready."

That compliment replayed on Jones's mind all day. When he left the clinic, he was so excited he needed to let out some steam. He missed New York. The easy access to gay clubs. Their liberal minds. This was the South, where people were discriminated against and beaten up for much less. He needed to be careful. But tonight, his body was aching for a man's touch, and he would get it.

New in the city, having no friends or favorite places to frequent, Peter Brown passed by The Wilken Institute around six p.m. whenever he wasn't working at the hospital. That was when most of the medical staff left, except for Richard, who went home between six thirty and seven. Peter enjoyed seeing Richard even from a distance. He'd had a lot of practice doing so since they were residents.

Richard had been so distant then. Polite, but painfully unreachable. What a joy it had been experiencing his warm treatment the evening they'd met at that bar. Peter had approached him almost fearfully, just to test his courage, and Richard had suggested getting a table to chat.

It had meant so much, but Peter had to decline and run away before he said or did something stupid. He'd been in love with Richard for seven years. A platonic, ridiculous love he had done everything to fight against. Had slept with half of Boston fighting against. All in vain.

Love was a lethal virus from which one could not escape. Almost as lethal as the one silently inhabiting Peter's body. It was a question of time until he started feeling the symptoms, showing the signs, and if he wasn't popular before, with AIDS, he would die alone.

Maybe that AZT novelty he was taking would work. More likely, his days were numbered. That's why Peter came to Houston and felt freer than ever. He could surprise Richard with a kiss next time they met; he could kill his wife to later comfort him. Finally, he could do whatever the fuck he wanted.

Peter had followed some of the doctors from The Wilken Institute trying to see who he could casually befriend to get him close to Richard.

So far, Dr. Dario Sullivan had been his best shot. A family man, Sullivan often stopped at a pizza place after work. Peter followed him inside one evening and placed a random order.

As they waited, Peter made small talk and let Sullivan know he was an anesthesiologist.

"Crazy small world!" Sullivan said. "Me too. I work at The Wilken Institute."

*Bingo!* "It's wonderful to meet a colleague. I went to Harvard and moved here recently to work at Mercy. Great job, but the hours are insane. For the right salary, I'd rather do what you're doing."

"That may be possible—Wilken went to Harvard too. Do you know him?"

"Superficially."

Sullivan's pizzas were ready, and he got up to get

them. "Why don't you give him a call? We hired more surgeons and could use another hand in anesthesia."

"Thanks for the tip! I'll think about it."

Peter didn't need to think. Jobs and money meant nothing to him now. He didn't want to make that call. He wanted Richard to call him.

It had been four days since he met Sullivan and the call hadn't happened, so either that idiot hadn't mentioned his name or Richard didn't want to work with him.

The second option was as heartbreaking as every time Peter had invited Richard to do anything in Boston and gotten no as an answer, no matter if it was for lunch, drinks, or even discussing a case. They say we obsess over what we can't have and hell, it was true. Only this time, Peter was going to have it.

A new face was heading to the parking lot, tall and lean like Peter liked them. Young too, with short red hair, some three years his junior. Two years Richard's junior. He could be one of the new surgeons. He could be a patient. Since Peter had nothing better to do, anything was game. If Baby Face were, in fact, a new surgeon, he probably wouldn't have a wife and kids to buy pizza for, and they might be able to talk longer than he had talked to Sullivan.

Peter followed the stranger's car hoping he would stop at a bar or restaurant and he could follow him inside. The man stopped at a modest shopping center with no places to eat or drink, and Peter's gut told him to wait in the parking lot in case the stranger was there for a quick pick-up and came back too quickly for Peter to return to his car.

Peter waited, and short of half an hour later, another man approached the stranger's car. Initially Peter thought the man was trying to break into the car. Then he laughed. *No...*

Peter wasn't close enough to be certain, but when the stranger got the keys out of his pocket and opened the car, Peter knew it was the same man in disguise.

*Interesting.*

Peter continued to follow the car, and when the man started heading outside the city, he had a feeling of where he might be going. He'd heard of the place, just had no interest in checking it out. His stock of energy was limited now. He needed to use it wisely.

In aviator glasses, a black T-shirt, and a bucket hat concealing his very identifiable red hair, Mark Jones felt excited entering the only gay bar in Houston his New York friends had recommended as reasonably safe. He'd sworn that in that new city he would focus on his plan and stay away from trouble. What was he thinking? That he'd marry a southern belle and have a bunch of children? His mother would have loved that. He might have loved the simplicity of that. It just wasn't possible.

Tomorrow he would go back to real life and more meaningful goals. Tonight he was here to take it all in. The loud music, the hypnotizing blinking lights, the artificial fog masking a dance floor filled with danger and irresistible fun.

The smell of beer spilled on the wood floor was a reminder of a certain Irish pub with spacious restrooms, the face that materialized beside him one of the men he fucked there.

"I'm Peter," the stranger said. "Can I buy you a drink?"

# 19

THE PARTY INCLUDED the entire staff of The Wilken Institute of Plastic Surgery. Among doctors, nurses, and administrative staff, a total of thirty-two heads gathered around the pool enjoying drinks and a generous buffet with seafood, salads, smoked ham, and fresh pasta. As usual, Timothy and Victoria were present.

Before joining the others, Dr. Moore grabbed a glass of champagne and walked around the property. This was the house where he should be living. Moore was certain that he would have been on the same TV shows and magazine covers as Richard had he married a Texan heir who bought him a luxury clinic. In Boston, he had no less brains or talents than Richard. His former classmate—now boss—just had always been a man capable of anything to reach his goals. No principles. No loyalty. Moore was ready to do the same.

It was a shame someone would have to die for his happiness.

When everyone had arrived, Richard dinged a spoon to his glass asking for everyone's attention. "I'd like to thank you for joining me and my wife, Constance, at our home. In these past years, you have done so much for the institute, and I'd like to let you know that you're here because I consider you family."

Everyone applauded and Samantha found her hands following. Richard was enchanting. For the first time in her career, she hadn't seen one employee complain about their boss. "Dr. Wilken is nice." "Dr. Wilken is generous." "Dr. Wilken is polite." The worst she had heard related to the man was "Dr. Wilken's wife is a bitch."

Never a bad word about Richard himself and still, Sam was certain there should be a reason why Constance called her every week inquiring about her husband's schedule and how many surgeries he'd performed. *Had he cheated? Was that about how much money he was bringing to their business?*

Being divorced, childless, and the only daughter of deceased parents, Sam experienced enormous freedom. Sometimes she wished she had more of a personal life so she didn't have to play mother at work, putting everyone in The Wilken Institute under a microscope like their problems were also hers.

*Mind your own business*, Sam told herself, finishing her mimosa. Her eyes betrayed her and she looked at the Wilkens again. Both smiling; Richard's arm around Constance's shoulder, posing for a photograph.

Samantha did not sense the love Richard was supposed to feel for his pregnant wife. *Something is very wrong in this marriage.*

Richard introduced his in-laws to those who still didn't know them and talked about how excited they all were about the baby's arrival. He raised his glass. "Feel free to walk around the property, and have fun!"

Tyler came straight to the Carltons. Shook Timothy's hand and kissed Victoria's. "This reminds me of the evening I met Richard," Victoria said. "You're like him, handsome and charming. I'm glad things worked out about the job."

"Entirely because of you!"

"My pleasure. And thank you for the flowers."

"It was the least I could do."

"Have you met my daughter?"

"I've seen her in the clinic once, but we haven't met yet."

"Come. I'll introduce you."

Constance had finished greeting a group of guests and Victoria said, "Honey, this is Dr. Tyler MacLaine."

"Oh, Richard talks a lot about you. Nice to meet you."

"Nice to meet you too."

At seven months, Constance's belly was exploding. Even though she liked parties, moving around was becoming challenging. "Guys, I need to sit down."

All the tables were taken. Some had two people

engaged in animated conversations, and others had five or six chairs squeezed in to fit a big group.

Tyler knew that anyone would jump up in a heartbeat for the pregnant wife of their boss to have a seat, but he saw an opportunity to show initiative. "Hold on a second," he told Constance.

He approached a group of nurses with a smile as bright as the sun above him and talked to them for a minute. They nodded and looked at Constance and her parents, making hand gestures for them to come take their seats.

"Thank you, ladies," Tyler said. "I owe you one."

As the women walked away and joined their colleagues across the pool, Constance said, "You know how to get things your way, Tyler. I like that."

Louise stopped by to bring Constance's apple juice and vitamin capsules. "Do you need anything else?" the multitasking assistant asked.

"Please bring my baby. He must be tired of being locked up." As Louise left, Constance turned back to Tyler. "My baby chimpanzee. A friend of mine knew this man in Hollywood who owned several wild animals." And she began to tell Tyler about how George ended up in her life.

When George actually showed up and moved from Louise's arms to Constance's lap, everyone at the party stopped to look at them. Most of the employees knew Constance was eccentric. What they hadn't heard of was her exotic pet. George looked adorable wearing a blue bow tie and hat, and people couldn't help coming closer to see him. "Can I pat him, Mrs. Wilken?" asked one of the nurses, and several hands followed.

One hour later, George had become the king of the party and had sat on a dozen laps.

Samantha did not join "Ape World." She had talked a bit with her office staff, then with the doctors and nurses. She tried to relax, but clearly this was work on a Saturday when she could be doing something else. Anything that didn't require wearing spandex identical to the ones their patients wore after abdominal surgery to make her look skinnier in her summer dress.

Sam was at the buffet deciding what she could eat without getting sick with the pressure in her stomach. Three spoons of salad, a couple of shrimps. She adored crab legs. It wouldn't be ladylike eating them in public though. She would die for a single spoon of the mushroom pasta. There just wasn't much extra room for her size-six spandex to actually expand.

She noticed Richard coming toward her and planned to head back to her table.

He was faster. "There's more food inside."

She laughed with him. "Not very hungry."

He got a plate for himself and started to fill it. "It's always like this, right? Those who should be on a diet can't do it, and the skinny ones don't like to eat."

"I'm not that skinny, Dr. Wilken, and pushing forty, I have to start watching my back."

"You're right. But live a little. Don't forget you can have free cosmetic surgery anytime you want."

He left with a smile and Samantha stood there, impressed that her mysterious boss could be that generous.

Mark Jones held his glass of wine and smiled at his colleagues as they told their tales in the operating room. His mind was on Peter Brown. Would the universe be that benevolent, providing his dream man exactly when he was about to give up finding him?

Like him, Peter was an Ivy League doctor, smart and only older enough to sound wiser. Peter had also just moved to Houston and didn't know anyone in town. They discovered so many common interests. So many things to explore together. And God, the sex was fabulous!

Jones so desperately wanted to have Peter around today. They could be together in the most discreet fashion while they grew their very promising careers. Peter looked very manly. They could easily live together and pass as roommates.

Jones felt blessed and laughed easily at whatever stories his colleagues were telling. He was barely listening and still scoring points as a pleasant guy to hang out with.

He tried not to look at his watch every five minutes. It was a quarter past noon, and he said he would call Peter at one.

Finally, he saw Richard walk inside the house alone and followed him. Richard crossed the enormous living room and disappeared with a left turn into a hallway.

Jones waited. One of the receptionists of the Institute passed by him and asked, "Is the restroom that way?"

He nodded. Homes that big had a dozen bathrooms. There must be one around the area the young lady headed to. Richard returned and before he asked anything, Jones said, "I know today's not about work, but would you have a moment?"

"Of course. Can we talk here?"

"Sure. Nothing secretive."

The two sat at the couch and Jones said, "I was wondering if with two extra surgeons, you would consider hiring another anesthesiologist. I have a friend who would be a great acquisition to the clinic."

"It's a possibility. I spoke to Sullivan about it. Is your friend from Columbia as well?"

"No, he's here and he went to Harvard with you. Peter Brown."

Richard remembered his brief encounter with Peter Brown at the bar of the St. Regis. "Yeah, he told me he was working for Mercy."

"He is, but he would prefer working more regular hours, so if you're hiring, he'd be happy to join our team."

At Harvard, Peter Brown didn't strike Richard as what he would call *a great acquisition* to his clinic. He was good enough, but if Richard could never remember the man's name, he wasn't hiring material. "Thank you, Jones. Brown's a great guy. I'm just not sure about this." He patted Jones on the shoulder. "Let's go back to the party."

Even though Brain was a patient man, his patience had stretched thin.

Constance was on the cover of *Parents* magazine. She was so huge in that yellow dress that production should have given her something else to wear, or the editor should have vetted the photo.

It must be nice being a millionaire. Even Richard was for sale.

Brain wouldn't burn that photo. He hung it on the fridge with a magnet and stared at Constance as he stirred his tea. He hated coffee, the memories it resurrected. Even the smell of it made him nauseous.

With her pregnancy, Constance had detoured Brain's plan like she'd done in Boston years ago. At that time, he'd simply wanted her to have a drop of dignity and break up with Richard. He tried to warn her about the affair with his anonymous letter. When Constance did nothing, he involved Sally's husband.

Proud Dr. John Landry would leave a cheating wife. What Brain wasn't sure about was what the man would do if he learned about the affair in advance or caught Richard and Sally in the act. Somebody could get hurt, and Brain simply wanted the cheaters to be unmasked. His anonymous call wouldn't prepare Landry for what he was going to find, and Brain would stick around in case things got out of control.

That was a perfect evening to put his plan into action. Brain was familiar with the lovers' routine. About three shameless hours spent at Sally's home, usually from seven to ten p.m. Then Richard left from the back door, crossed the poorly lit backyard, and walked to the subway station. From his hidden place near Sally's home, Brain watched. He gave the lovers time for their sins and made the call around nine so Landry would arrive when Richard was about to leave.

Surprisingly, Richard left Sally's place earlier than usual, seeming nervous.

Soon afterward, John Landry arrived. No one entered the house in the meantime.

Brain heard a scream and Landry came outside wailing. Hiding in the dark, Brain stood frozen smelling the scent of death. There'd been no need to go inside to know Sally had been murdered.

# 20

CONSTANCE'S CONTRACTIONS STARTED getting strong at 2:20 a.m., and they went to the hospital. A few hours into a labor Constance swore would be intervention-free, she was begging for a needle to her spine. "I can't take this!"

Alternating crying and screaming, she talked to the baby. "I'm sorry! I didn't want to pollute your blood!"

Richard held her hand. "The baby will be fine with the epidural."

"So get me one!"

"I'll check with the doctor on duty," the nurse said, "Your ob-gyn hasn't arrived yet."

As if on cue, Dr. Claire Simmons appeared at the door and Constance breathed a sigh of relief. "Thank God you're here. This isn't working. I'm gonna die!"

Dr. Simmons looked at Richard and by their silent

communication, she knew everything was going according to what nature had determined. "I know it's tough, darling, but nothing's wrong."

"She changed her mind about the epidural," Richard said.

Dr. Simmons nodded. "They all do. I'll get it for you."

Peter Brown was all smiles when he entered Constance's room. "Mrs. Wilken, I'm the anesthesiologist. Let's get the agony out of this beautiful moment."

It had completely escaped Richard's mind that Brown worked there. "Hi, Peter," he said. "Good to see you."

"Good to see you, Richard." He turned back to Constance. "I'll ask you to please sit up, Mrs. Wilken, arch your back and remain still until I tell you, okay?"

"I'll try."

"You're doing great. Sometimes when I get to the room, the patient has already torn off her clothes."

Constance chuckled.

"Would you mind helping her, Richard?"

Everything changed the second the needle penetrated her skin. The contractions slowed down and Constance lay back in her bed.

"Better?" Peter asked.

Constance liked his smile. "A lot better. Thank you!"

"That's my job."

"No, for being so sweet."

"I consider that my job too."

"Thank you, man," Richard said.

"Any time. And all the best to you both and your baby."

Measuring nineteen inches long and weighing 6.8 pounds, Adam Carlton Wilken claimed his place in the world with a loud cry. Holding Adam in his arms was even more powerful for Richard than meeting him during that first sonogram. This time, Richard did not cry. He had talked to Adam every day, monitored his growth twice a month, and looked in his eyes multiple times on a screen. This was the live version of a miracle that had started months ago. Adam was the first person Richard felt connected to. Adam was his tribe and his new reason to exist.

Richard was admiring his son when Adam's lips curved up in a half moon. "He smiled at me!"

Constance barely looked at them. "Oh, it's probably gas. God, I'm exhausted. Can he come back later?"

Richard's eyes stayed on Adam and he hoped his son could really read his mind. *You don't need her. I'll take care of you.*

Richard was planning two weeks away from the clinic. Ultimately, he decided to stay home a month. For Constance, Adam was a sophisticated doll she liked to dress up and show off to her friends. She never changed a diaper and made no efforts to breastfeed.

"That's nonnegotiable," Richard said. "Maternal milk is essential for the baby's immune system."

"It hurts like shit! And with my history, I probably don't even have much milk."

"Your breasts are fully functional, Constance. Dr. Simmons examined you and your glands were never affected by your surgeries."

"That's crazy! My boobs never did their job when I needed them. Now they won't malfunction so I can have a break?"

The middle ground was using a breast pump several times a day and the nanny would feed the infant with a bottle. One day Richard told the woman, "Let me try."

Yolanda loved men who cared for their children. Especially important men who hired help to do so. "Of course, sir." She transferred Adam to Richard's arms. "He prefers to lie on the left arm. Not sure why."

"I'll remember that."

The two exchanged smiles and Yolanda gave the bottle to Richard, showing him the best angle, and when Adam was finished, how to make him burp.

Richard never thought those trivial steps could hold such fascination. While he was home, he bathed and fed Adam almost every day and spent hours observing the boy's motor and mental development.

Constance enjoyed dancing around with the baby to make him laugh. Then she handed him to the nanny and went shopping. Adam's closet was overflowing with new outfits and his bedroom with expensive toys.

The day before Richard returned to work, Constance woke up in the middle of the night and didn't find him. The nursery lights were on, and she quietly opened the door.

Richard was sitting in the rocking chair with Adam curled in the crook of his arm. Both asleep. Constance almost cried. She had never seen Richard so vulnerable. So giving. Maybe he was becoming the man she always wanted him to be.

She walked over to Richard and gently patted him on the shoulder. He opened his eyes slowly like a man who'd been lost in blissful sleep.

He looked up and Constance smiled, then signaled for him to put the baby in bed.

Richard got up and carefully laid Adam in his cradle, covering him with a light blanket.

"He's such an angel," Constance whispered.

"Yeah, I'll miss spending my days with you both."

Richard's face was so serene, his eyes as sincere as when she first met him. In the dimmed lights of that blue room that smelled like baby powder, Constance felt her old wounds begin to heal.

# 21

A YEAR AGO, Brain had to comb the newspapers and magazines to get something on Richard Wilken. Sometimes he and Constance appeared in social columns attending a gala or on a trip abroad. Their wedding had been covered by important media in the South, followed by photos of their honeymoon a few weeks later.

Now, their faces were everywhere. Brain could endure no more pictures of the couple with their baby. He chose to clip one photo of Richard alone holding Adam. How incredible that a still image could capture so much love.

He could have killed Constance during her gestation, but what kind of a monster would he be if he'd killed a baby? He wished Constance had died during labor. How many times he saw it happen during medical school.

The universe just knew he had to be the one to kill her.

Richard returned to work and asked Samantha to schedule his surgeries so they would always end before four p.m. and he could get home in time to put Adam to sleep. One afternoon, when the child had turned two months old, Richard arrived home earlier and, not finding anyone downstairs, headed to the nursery.

He stopped abruptly at the door. Constance was holding George near the cradle, allowing the chimpanzee to caress Adam's face.

Richard felt like his lungs had given up on him. Afraid to scare the animal, he didn't make a sound until Constance saw him.

"See?" she said, "I told you they'd be like brothers."

"Please take him away," Richard said in the lowest, calmest voice he could mutter.

"Oh, Richard. You're such a party pooper."

When both George's hands were around Constance's neck and she was standing far enough from his son, Richard said, "Can you follow me, please?"

With a long sigh, Constance left the room, and when the door was firmly closed, Richard said, "Are you out of your fucking mind?"

Constance rolled her eyes. "Don't be so dramatic. I'm watching them. Nothing will happen."

He pointed at George. "In case you haven't noticed, this is not another child. He can hurt Adam in a second and you'd be able to do nothing but watch."

"I never told you because I knew that's how you'd react."

"Do you think I'm wrong?"

"Yes. George visits Adam every day when you're not here. He's used to him."

Richard made an enormous effort not to slap Constance, and he felt like screaming, *If you don't get rid of this monkey, I will!* That wasn't the effective way to communicate with his crazy wife, though. Soon, she and that furry nightmare would be out of his life. *Breathe.*

He tried to imprint sympathy in his face. "I know you love George. The question is, do you love him more than me?"

Constance caressed the chimpanzee's back. "He gives me a lot more attention. You're either at work or with Adam."

Richard managed a smile. "You said the baby would save our marriage, and he's doing that. You and I will spend more time together—just promise me that George will stay outside."

That week, a seven-hundred-square-foot wooden house was built around the garden for George. It was as comfortable as a human home, with beds and couches and sophisticated toys designed for wild creatures living in sanctuaries. The only feature Constance disapproved of was the fence impeding George's access to the family's mansion. It was there because she had promised Richard, and since then, he had become more attentive to her.

Constance split her time between the two homes, and if she were honest, she was spending more time with George than with Adam. The baby had Richard. The two loved each other, and even though Adam didn't speak yet, they had their own dialect from which she was invariably left out.

Richard would come from work, have a quick shower, and go spend time with Adam. One day, Constance surprised Richard showing up naked in the bathroom. She stepped into the running water and rubbed the soap on his chest. He fucked her so robotically, she faked an orgasm so he could rush to his son.

Constance didn't want George to feel abandoned like she did. His big yellow eyes seemed often sad, like she had betrayed him, replaced him with her new son.

Why couldn't Richard understand that she was perfectly capable of handling things when he wasn't around?

Peter Brown still hadn't swallowed Richard's refusing to hire him. And the fact that he didn't reconsider, even after Peter's sweet performance at the hospital during the baby's birth. Impressive how love could so easily turn into hatred and often back to love at the slightest warm gesture. Peter had been on that road long enough to know.

Tonight, he was particularly angry. At Richard and at stupid Mark Jones, who hadn't been a good advocate. Jones was below him moaning against the pillow as Peter penetrated him from behind. Peter had asked

Jones to stay that way so he could fantasize he was fucking Richard.

Normally in Peter's fantasies, Richard was the one penetrating him. The man was too dominant to be a bottom, and Peter would come in seconds imagining Richard inside him.

Right now, he just wanted to punish Richard and make him feel small. Why had Richard always been so indifferent? What had he done for Richard to consider even his intellectual power below his own?

Pain was the key. Richard would be more humble if he hurt like Peter did.

Peter closed his eyes, and as he moved deeper and faster into Jones's body, he also immersed into his fantasy. His hands traveled from Richard's hips to his shoulders, and he squeezed them hard.

Richard's moan filled the room with a mix of pleasure and pain, and knowing that Richard could hear his thoughts, Peter said, *No pleasure. Just pain.* His moves became rougher.

That game was a turnoff for Jones. Peter was hurting his shoulders, fingernails making imprints on his skin. That was a novelty, but Jones went on with it, assuming Peter was close to his climax. He continued to moan and call Peter's name, hoping to accelerate the process.

Hearing Richard call his name as if he were begging for mercy did increase Peter's excitement. His power. The whip hidden in the back of his closet would make a beautiful mark on that fair skin. A shame he hadn't brought it.

Peter grabbed Richard by the hair and yanked his head back as his other hand scratched him from neck to waist. *Close enough to a whip mark.*

Peter would have climaxed if Jones hadn't rolled over and pushed him away. "Where the fuck are you?"

# 22

RICHARD INTENDED TO wait until Adam was six months old to resume his plan of ending Constance's life. This way, she could breastfeed without psychiatric drugs in her system. Or at least, not more than the minimal amount she took during the gestation.

Constance was determined to get her body back to its prepregnancy state and went to Richard for more plastic surgery. "I'd go back to Ivo for my breasts," she said, meaning Dr. Pitanguy, "but it would be silly going to Brazil only to lift them a bit."

"I don't think you should touch the breasts," Richard said. "You know this is fragile territory, and they look awesome."

"They used to. Breastfeeding ruined them."

"Well, you're almost done with your motherly

duties and will be able to do everything you want in a few months."

"Months? I look awful! Even my face seems so old!"

"You just had a baby, darling. You can't do anything big now."

Constance examined herself in the mirror and then said, "So, I want cheek implants."

"You don't need that."

"Shit, why do we own a plastic surgery clinic if I can't use it to become prettier?"

Richard pretended not to hear her.

"I'm serious. I wanna do at least my cheeks, and I want you to do them."

"I said I would never operate on you. You want to do facial, it'll be Jones or Tyler."

She sighed. "You can be pretty useless. Okay. Talk to Jones. I wanna do it next week."

The surgery went well. During recovery a nurse tended to Constance, and two nannies switched shifts to care for Adam. The good news was that recovery from cheek implants was reasonably fast. In the first days, Constance felt a stretched, tight sensation in the cheek area that subsided in a week. There was still swelling and redness, and Constance felt like crying if she looked in the mirror. *You'll be prettier*, she told herself. *Stay strong.*

Her mantra was not powerful enough. Richard was working and she went to Adam's room. The baby smiled at her, and she didn't know if it was because he loved her or because of her remaining swelling and redness. Maybe like all men in her life, Adam would find her ugly or not enough. He had Richard's DNA, after all. How much would that kid be predisposed to love her?

She held Adam in her arms for a while, bouncing him around the room, and then stooped by the window, where she could see the garden and George's new home.

Her heart ached with remorse. No one loved her more than George. No one enjoyed more of her company. She hadn't seeing him in a week because of the risks of infection, but damn it, she had healed enough, and seeing George would offer her heart a more essential type of healing.

Richard was in the middle of a procedure when the phone in the operating room started ringing nonstop. That was unusual and a nurse took it quickly. The woman's face went pale. "Right away." She turned to Richard. "Dr. Wilken, your nanny asked you to go home. There's an emergency involving your son."

The woman on the operating table was a famous singer. One that if something went wrong could ruin Richard's reputation. Nothing of that crossed his mind when he dropped the scalpel. "Page Jones and send 911 to my place."

Richard peeled off his scrubs and rushed to the parking lot. There was no point calling to learn details. He just needed to be there. Mercifully, it wasn't rush hour and he made it home in twenty minutes.

When he turned onto his street and saw the police car and the fire truck, he thought of Adam trapped in a room in flames because of Constance's damn scented candles. He left the car and ran inside.

His property was a war zone with dozens of people in different uniforms moving about. A police officer came to him, his voice loud and tense, and said, "Mr. Wilken?"

"Yes, what happened?"

"Your chimpanzee attacked your wife and took your baby inside its house. We're trying to lure him out, but we may have better luck with your help."

Richard had trouble making sense of the words. "There's a fence keeping the chimp outside. How'd it happen?"

"Your wife took the baby there, sir."

Richard ran behind the policeman toward George's house. When they arrived, the firefighters had put a hook on the doorknob to keep it open. George was holding the baby and was very agitated. There was no way to shoot a dart with sedatives without risking Adam's life. After frantic efforts to lure the animal with food and toys, everyone backed up until Richard arrived.

"I'm here!" Richard said, heading to the door.

"I wanna help too!"

Richard caught sight of Constance, face bleeding from what seemed to be a bite, crying and begging the paramedics to let her in. Richard would kill her if she approached his son again. He advanced slowly, his legs so weak he thought they wouldn't bear his weight.

George was in the back holding Adam like a doll against his chest. Richard hoped he wasn't too late. His son was mute.

"George," Richard said very low. "It's all right."

George looked at him suspiciously. He glanced outside, saw the strangers staring at him. He hissed and Adam started crying.

Richard could breathe again. *Stay strong, son. You'll tell it to your children one day.*

Richard got on his knees. "Shhhhhhh. It's okay." And he was talking to both Adam and George. Neither seemed to be soothed by him. The baby continued to cry, and George ran to the other room. Richard ran after them and in seconds, George had climbed up the wooden tree Constance had designed for him. It had several platforms from floor to ceiling so George could exercise.

The chimp climbed up with one arm, carrying Adam with the other.

Richard stepped back and shouted to the firefighters, "He's headed to the ceiling! We'll need a net here."

Richard started to climb toward the first platform, and as he reached it, George went up one more level. Richard stopped. *God, if you exist, please show me what to do!*

Almost as quickly as George had made his way up, the rescue team spread a large net and six men tied it in place. It was still a long fall. Thirty feet. Richard had to get up there himself.

Slowly, he made his way to the second platform,

and this time, George stayed in place. Adam never ceased crying. Richard put his hand in his pocket and retrieved his keyring. "Here. Let's exchange toys." As George looked at the flashy blue stone, Richard advanced slowly to the next platform. George didn't move, and Richard smiled at him. "Good boy." He tried to make his voice sing-songy and friendly.

Richard continued his slow advance, firefighters immobile, eyes glued on him. He reached the third platform and the fourth. He was only three levels below them and started singing a Dutch lullaby Adam slept to.

After a moment, the baby stopped crying and even George seemed calmer.

*This will work!* Singing softly and advancing very, very slowly, Richard went up one more level. He had to be extremely careful now. Richard continued climbing, eyes on Adam, heart high in his throat.

"Where's my baby?" Constance's scream exploded in the room. "Ungrateful motherfucker!" she yelled at George. "I trusted you!"

Heavy footsteps followed. "You need to get out, ma'am."

"Nooooooo!"

As two men grabbed Constance to drag her out, George jumped down to defend her. Before he did, he let go of Adam.

It happened too fast. Richard tried an impossible jump to grab the baby, but he was too far. Adam was falling and three firemen instinctively moved forward to try to catch him. One of them might have if the boy's head hadn't hit one of the lower platforms. He was dead before he touched the net.

Constance's scream fused with Richard's, and for the first time, they had something in common. A pain so profound their chests were tearing. A hopelessness so deep they both fell on their knees.

After the tears came the rage. While the firefighters captured George and put him in a cage, Richard climbed down so fast his hands burned with the friction against the wood.

"You crazy bitch! He should have killed you!" He rushed toward Constance, ready to tear off the rest of her face, and a strong man from the rescue team restrained him. Richard continued to scream, "How many times did I warn you?"

# 23

THE BRIGHT SPRING morning with cloudless blue skies seemed appropriate for a child's funeral. Mother Nature's homage to someone who had left long before he could enjoy its beauty.

Richard stood beside Timothy and Victoria to his right, and Tyler to his left. The two doctors had grown closer over the past few days. Tyler had shown up at the house as soon as he heard of the tragedy and offered his shoulder when Richard broke down.

Constance couldn't attend the funeral. Consumed by guilt, she was a suicide threat again and would remain in a psychiatric clinic until Dr. Kessler decided it was safe for her to go home. How ironic that Constance had gotten to exactly the mental place Richard had wanted, but for a price he never intended to pay.

After the funeral, there was no reception. They

would make a memorial when Constance felt better. "Let me know if you need anything," Dr. Stein told Richard. One by one, the other doctors shook his hand and murmured sympathies.

Samantha and the rest of the staff nodded and kept a respectful distance.

"Are you sure you don't want company?" Tyler asked Richard. "You shouldn't be alone."

"Yeah. I'll see you tomorrow at work."

"Tomorrow? You're not doing that!"

"It'll help me forget."


On the way to his bedroom, Richard passed the nursery. The blue elephant painted on the door. He couldn't gather the strength to go in. He took a pill and slept for seventeen hours.

He awoke thirsty, as if his body had dehydrated out of weeping. The long corridor was dark except for the moonlight filtering through the glass ceiling like a blue veil guiding his way. Such a beautiful house filled with so much unhappiness.

Richard was certain that Adam's death had been a punishment for his crimes. He wanted to run away, leaving even the clothes on his body behind. Despite so much wealth, he had no freedom. With those compromising photos of him and Sally Landry, Constance still held the key to his cell. Long ago, Richard had agreed to play that game. With Adam gone, his old ambitions had lost their luster.

If Constance walked through those doors now, he

would kill her with his own hands in front of a hundred witnesses. He couldn't see that hatred being tamed. That could happen tomorrow, next week, or in a month, and he would happily go to jail, so why wait?

He went to his studio, sat at his desk, and picked out a sheet of fancy stationary, the header of which read, "Wilken Institute of Plastic Surgery. From the desk of Dr. Richard Wilken."

He stared at the paper and the Mont Blanc in his hand. There would be no return from this. Richard took a deep breath. *There's no return from anything.*

Pen on paper, the words came quickly.

*To Detective Berman*

*Boston PD*

*Regarding the Sally Landry's case – January of 1986.*

And he began writing his confession letter.

# 24

RICHARD COULD FEEL the heavy eyes on him as he arrived at the Institute the following morning. It started with the valet and the security guard. Both receptionists, trained to smile at anything that moved, started curving their lips at Richard and froze midway as if, despite being in their twenties, their cheeks were saturated with Botox.

They wished him good morning and looked down at their desks.

As Constance had once described, the Institute truly looked like a fancy hotel. Behind the reception desk was a circular free area with plants and seats, like a sophisticated indoor plaza. There were offices around it, and from there, one could see the mezzanines of the other three floors. The roof, like the Wilkens' house, was made of glass and steel, creating a modern look and filling the place with natural light.

Samantha's eyes followed Richard from the entrance to the elevator. Each of his steps seemed to weigh a ton, and if Samantha disliked Constance before, she now hated the woman. What kind of mother put her child's life in danger like that?

"Poor boss," Sam's secretary said. "I never understood why terrible things happen to great people."

The financial officer laughed. "That's why I don't go to church."

"Shhh," Samantha said without deviating her gaze. "Today is not a day for jokes."

Unlike the others, who could hide, Sam had urgent business with Richard. She wished someone else had been assigned to make decisions that week. She had a pop star's manager calling every other minute to know what would happen to their surgery scheduled the following day. It wasn't a subject to be discussed on the phone, and Sam slowly made her way to Richard's office.

A gentle knock and Richard asked her to come in. He looked more present, which she considered a great deed since the funeral had happened twenty-four hours ago. It would be stupid to ask how he was doing. Sam went straight to the point. "I hate to bother you, Dr. Wilken, but here's the situation."

She explained the pop star's expectations and concerns and Richard said, "Tell him I'm back and ready to do it as planned, unless he prefers Jones or Tyler to do it. Let the client decide."

"His manager said if you were well, he'd rather have you. They just wanted a word with you later today."

"It's settled then. I'll call him."

"Thank you."

Back to her office, Samantha resolved half a dozen other issues, but Richard's cool was eating at her all day. It was impossible that his nerves were in the right place. What if he made a mistake tomorrow?

She went home thinking about it and had a dreadful night of sleep.

The Institute had a helipad to provide VIP clients an extra layer of discretion. The pop star arrived at seven a.m., and the early hours combined with the fasting made him a lot less fun than he was onstage.

"Don't you think you're pushing yourself?" Tyler asked Richard.

"The higher the stakes, the more focused I'll be."

Tyler thought Richard was being a fool. Why play Superman when he felt shitty and shouldn't be taking risks? But he had become the new friend Richard's entire family adored. Better keep his mouth shut. "That's what you told the client?" he joked.

"Kind of." A faint smiled tinted Richard's lips. "Thank you for having my back, Tyler. I won't forget."

The surgery was over before noon and everything went well. Samantha relaxed. Three other important surgeries were scheduled for next week, and she worked until after seven that night to get the paperwork ready. Everyone else seemed to be gone except for Dr. Moore's team, who were wrapping up their last surgery. She would drop those folders at each doctor's office and head home. Her last stop was Richard's, and when she entered, he was sitting at his desk crying.

"Sorry! I thought you were gone."

Richard didn't try to disguise it. He just stared at Sam and she backed off and closed the door.

Outside, she put a hand on her face. "Shit."

Sam waited a moment and then knocked, but went in before Richard replied. "I don't know what to say, Dr. Wilken. Is there anything I can do, other than knocking before barging in?"

Richard had wiped his tears and pulled himself together. "It's not your fault. I've been leaving early for months…only now, there's no reason to."

Richard was looking at a framed photo of Constance, Adam, and himself. "He was a gorgeous boy, wasn't he?"

Constance's face had been torn out of the picture. "Absolutely," Sam said.

"During the funeral, I remembered a boy in my school who fell from a swing." Richard chuckled, his eyes brimming with tears again. "We were five-year-olds and thought only grandparents died."

"It should be that way. I lost my baby sister when I was in college, and I could think of nothing more unfair."

Richard looked at Sam as if meeting her for the first time. "You don't have children, right?"

"No, and the clock is ticking."

"Never wanted to?"

"Would love to, just never happened when I was married. Maybe I'll try solo one day."

"My dad used to say that having children changes you. He was right." Finally, Richard focused on the folder in Sam's hand. "Anything urgent?"

"Nothing you need to see until tomorrow."

"I'm in no rush to go home. I can take care of it now."

"If you'll stay, I can get you something to eat."

Sam returned with two sandwiches. "We've got chicken curry and smoked salmon."

"That's a lot better than the diet food patients are having upstairs."

"I try to keep the nurses happy too." Sam smiled. "Which one would you like?"

"Either. Thank you."

Sam put both options on Richard's desk and asked, "And to drink?"

"I need a martini."

She got something out of the fridge in his office. "Would a Diet Coke do? It tastes almost the same."

Richard found himself smiling. "I'll take your word for it."

On the following evening, Samantha brought Richard a trio of sandwiches to choose from. "I just couldn't sneak in the martini."

They had never talked about personal matters in over two years and suddenly, Samantha was as attentive as a long-time friend. "You're very kind," Richard said, "But please don't make this another task on your long list."

"It's not. I'm working late too, and if I'm getting myself a snack, it's no bother. Besides, I noticed you've lost some weight. I wanna make sure that you're eating at least a sandwich a day."

Richard laughed. "I'll tell you what. Why don't you eat here, and we'll discuss the subjects of the day?"

Along the next week, as they worked late and shared snacks, Richard discovered that Samantha Reeves was protective of whatever or whoever she cared about. That included the stray cats she fed still in her pajamas before coming to work and the old neighbor with whom she gardened on Saturdays, listening to stories he repeated every week.

"You should be working for charity," Richard told her. "A lot of people sign checks, but you have the heart for it."

"I'm not sure. I think I like those specific cats and that specific old man because they're my crowd."

"Your crowd?"

Samantha chuckled. "I better go back to work, boss. A few more of my silly comments and you'll start questioning my discernment to manage your company."

"Please tell me you have other friends," Richard teased.

"I do. We go out for beers and karaoke, but none of them took care of me when I had appendicitis. My old neighbor did."

While they went back to discussing VIP patients, Richard was still picturing Samantha's private life and her rare loyalties.

She was really something.

# 25

Constance stayed at the psychiatric clinic for forty-five days and only Victoria went to visit her. When Timothy learned about the circumstances of Adam's death, he was as indignant as Richard.

He screamed at Victoria, "You spoiled Connie her whole life and this baby's death is on you too! If it was up to me, our daughter would've been in a loony bin long ago!"

Victoria remained quiet anytime Timothy exploded on that subject. A father would never be as protective as a mother who had carried that life inside her, sharing every thought, feeling, and even her body's sustenance with the child.

Victoria had cried for Adam, but Constance was her baby.

"Stay with me for a while," Victoria told Constance when she was about to be released. "It'll be tough being home with so many memories."

"I no longer want to die, Mom. Don't worry."

Victoria sighed. "I also worry about you and Richard."

"He won't hurt me. He wasn't himself that day, and I deserved his rage."

"I'd like to stay there with you then."

"I'd like that."

Richard feared seeing Constance and not being able to control his anger. He focused on the night after Adam's funeral. The confession letter he had written. His second thoughts the following morning, and then the unexpected; and if not happy, life seemed tolerable again. No more slow-burn plans that always seemed to get detoured. Constance had left the clinic on a low suicidal risk. Those things changed. He had already replaced the contents of the dietary capsules she took three times a day with a cocktail of mood-altering drugs.

He would ensure that she ended her miserable life that week.

The limo stopped at the main entrance of their mansion and Constance got out of the backseat appearing ghostlike. She had mild psychiatric drugs in her system and was less lethargic than in her initial days in the clinic. Still, she was lifeless, deprived even of her obsessive vanity. Her precious hair was cut short again.

Constance looked at Richard standing by the door with a blank expression. "Hi."

"Hi." His voice was cold, and he said no more. He turned to Victoria, who left the car next, and was equally curt with her. "I'm going to work, just wanted to make sure you were all set."

Richard didn't allow the conversation to develop. He bid them good day and headed to his car.

"He hates me, Mom. He'll leave me."

"Do you think he's cheating again?"

Constance regretted that in a moment of weakness during one of her mother's recent visits at the psychiatric clinic, she'd told Victoria about Richard's affair back in Boston. Victoria was so angry that Constance cut the story short without revealing Sally's name, much less her murder. Unlike herself, who had used Richard's mistakes to blackmail him into the life she wanted, her mother was a woman who punished the wrong-doers. To Victoria, Richard had already become the enemy just by cheating. Imagine if she knew more? "Mom, he can't know that I told you. Promise me you won't say a thing?"

Victoria's eyes stayed on Richard's car disappearing outside the gate. "Don't worry, honey. You know how discreet I am."

For the next two days, Richard was merely cordial to his wife and mother-in-law. He moved to one of the guest rooms on a different floor from Constance's and had his meals alone either in the library or his studio.

On the third day, when he returned from the clinic and headed straight to his room, Constance followed him. "Can we talk, please?"

"I don't think there's much more for us to talk about." Richard made sure Victoria was not around and added, "I wouldn't be here if you hadn't kept me hostage."

"I know and that's what I wanna talk about." She showed him a familiar leather folder. "Please give me a minute."

They entered his room together and Constance said, "I know you can't even look at me, and I'm not here to ask for your forgiveness. What happened to Adam was my fault and I have to live with myself. But you don't have to."

She opened the folder and handed him an envelope and a stack of paperwork. "These are your photos with Sally, and these papers annul the agreements you signed. I have nothing against you anymore, Richard. I will never open my mouth about Sally and the money you'll make from now on is yours."

Richard was speechless and Constance continued, "What I took from you is far bigger than your cheating. I owe you this."

"So, I can divorce you without retaliation?"

"Yes, and you can keep the clinic. But I have a better offer."

"That seems fair enough."

"You were never a man who settled for enough, so hear me out."

Richard stared at her for a moment. "Go on."

"I know you hate me now, but what ha Adam changed me forever, and this time, w in the clinic, I really allowed them to treat showed him a report with the psychiatric cli "Look. This is a doctor's evaluation provin mentally sound. Lehman has a copy, so if we agreements, they will have legal effect."

Constance lowered her head. "Once you for a second chance when it seemed impossil to trust you. If you can do the same for me, a you is one year to prove that I can be a wonder

Richard wouldn't believe that possibilit God vouched for it himself. The only way C would become a wonderful wife was dead. I her offer was second best, and she was begg in the good old days, he could negotiate.

"I don't know, Constance. It never worked appreciate what you've done, but we're bette a divorce."

She came closer and raised her hand to c face but stopped. "Please, Richard. If you try, it worth your time."

"How?"

"Look at the last page."

Richard went through the document and af ing the clause Constance mentioned, he ask you serious?"

"Yes. If in one year we're not happy, I'll you willingly and give you half of everything

Constance had just saved her life.

# 26

ADAM'S MEMORIAL WAS held that weekend at the Wilkens' mansion. The family didn't have the heart to put a large photo of the baby on display. Instead, they made an altar with candles, a bowl of water representing serenity, and white lilies from Victoria's garden, symbolizing innocence. A mountain of letters and sympathy cards came from friends living in different parts of the world and even strangers who had read about their misfortune.

During Constance's absence, Richard had had her garden and George's house torn down and removed from his sight. She didn't say a word, and they agreed to hold the event inside. The pool area was too festive for something so sad.

The living room was populated by over a hundred relatives, friends, and clients of the Carltons, friends and colleagues of the Wilkens, and everyone from the

Institute. Most of the staff came accompanied by their significant others, except for Sam, one of the receptionists, and the financial officer. Tyler brought his new girlfriend, a paralegal from a local law firm. He introduced Linda to everyone and sat with Stein and his wife.

Jones brought someone he introduced as his good friend and colleague, Peter Brown.

"Good to see you again, Peter," said Dr. Sullivan, the anesthesiologist Peter had followed to the pizzeria. "A shame it's under such terrible circumstances."

"True. A tragedy."

"Did you ever call Richard about the job?"

So, Richard hadn't even mentioned anything to Sullivan. Peter smiled. "We actually met at the hospital when his wife was having the baby. But no, I'm enjoying my job now."

"Good to hear. It's a great hospital."

Lunch was served buffet style on a long table by the window. Some guests sat inside; others walked around the property carrying small plates.

Peter couldn't taste the food or pay attention to Jones's gibbering as they walked outside. He was in Richard's home. Not directly invited, but there, a part of his inner circle at last.

They arrived at the area where the garden used to be, and Jones said, "Here's where it happened." He shook his head as if trying to rid his mind of a terrifying memory. "It was ugly. I had recently done Constance's cheeks and they called me here to fix her face after the

210

paramedics sedated her. Richard was wild. He wouldn't let anyone near the baby, and Tyler was the one calming him down so he wouldn't have to be sedated as well."

Imagining Richard in such pain softened Peter's resentment. He wished he had been the friend there to comfort him. He didn't know Tyler. A face among dozens of introductions today. At that moment, Peter just hated the man for being important enough to Richard to have the power of taming him in a moment like that.

Peter could no longer tolerate Jones's company. He wanted to see more of the house. More of Richard's intimacy. "I need to use the restroom," he said. "And I'll walk around a little. We shouldn't be seen together all the time. Straight guys don't do that, remember?"

Jones smiled back at Peter. "You're right. It'll be good for you to hang out with these people. We'll talk tonight."

Drinks and hors d'oeuvres continued to be passed around while the guests talked and offered their sympathy to Constance and Richard. At some point everyone settled, and Timothy Carlton stood up to deliver a short speech. When he was finished, not one guest had dry eyes.

The media was not admitted. Even though several photographers were on standby outside the gates trying to flash important faces, they hadn't been lucky this time. Brain needed a photo for his collection, so he brought a small camera and earlier, from the privacy of a hallway, had managed a snapshot of Richard in his moment of pain.

He was outside now walking the vast lawn and enjoying a drink without the obligation of making conversation. He was still amazed at the size of the property and wanted to explore Richard's private life further. Seeing no one around, he entered a side door leading to a long hallway. As the main living area was at the end, he could hear the guests without seeing them. Even the air was different there, cozier, a part of the house reserved for few. Brain felt excited taking those steps.

Most doors were locked. The first that wasn't was the gym. He skipped it and tried the next doorknob. A playroom with a billiard table in the back. He was ready to try the third when he heard voices behind it. A man and a woman talking fast. He put his ear against the door, and their voices remained muffled by the thick wood. The woman was approaching the door now, and her voice was getting clearer. "I know. I love you too."

Brain left quickly and hid in the playroom. With the door a crack open, he saw the woman come out. Samantha Reeves. She was unaccompanied at the party, and the man inside did not follow her, which meant he was probably one of her married colleagues whose wife was down the hall eating canapés.

He waited, and almost ten minutes later Richard came out.

Brain smiled out of surprise, then turned serious. Samantha said she loved Richard. Was it possible that he loved her back?

That would be a game changer.

# 27

SAM WAS TALKING to the receptionists when Constance arrived at the clinic; Constance seemed almost as glamorous as she was before Adam's passing. Without any *hellos* or *good afternoons*, Constance said, "I'm going up. Is Richard in his office?"

"Yes, ma'am," said one receptionist. "I'll tell him you're on your way."

"Don't. It's a surprise."

Samantha tried to keep the smile on her face. Her cheeks trembled with the effort as Constance headed to the elevator.

"Bitch," one of the receptionists whispered, and her colleague laughed.

Samantha finished what she was saying and headed to her office, annoyed at her jealousy. *What is she doing here all dressed up, making surprises for Richard?*

213

Sam was too agitated to sit at her desk, so she went on her usual inspections up and down, growing gradually angrier as time passed, and Richard's door remained closed. She found excuses to stay on the second floor. Confirmed details of Tyler's surgery. Asked Moore about special supplies.

Finally the door opened and Constance and Richard headed to the elevator. They did not see Sam, and she watched as the couple walked side by side, talking and laughing. When the elevator door opened, Constance kissed Richard on the lips and walked in. Sam was flabbergasted. *What the fuck is going on?*

Richard's face fell as soon as the elevator doors closed, and Samantha realized something was wrong. When he turned and saw her, he made a discreet hand gesture for her not to go in his office now. They would talk after hours, as they had been doing the past two months.

Richard closed his door and leaned against it. He would love a drink but settled for a Diet Coke. He cracked a can open and filled a glass, the effervescent sound reminding him of pleasant evenings.

After Sally's murder, Richard had eliminated two things from his life: cocaine and cheating. What happened between Sam and him, however, didn't feel like cheating. It didn't even feel like his old conceptions of dating or sex. Sam understood loneliness and valued caring for people when they were down. Richard hadn't seen those altruistic qualities since he'd left the suburbs of Westchester.

A week after Adam's funeral, when Sam stopped by for what had become their seven p.m. meeting, Richard kissed her. For the first time, he wasn't being strategic about a woman. Kissing Sam was simply what he wanted. And she wanted it too. The next moment, they were on the couch, kissing, taking each other's clothes off.

When they were done, Richard regretted it. He thought of Constance and the mess that it could become.

Sam looked at him knowingly. "I'll never be another problem for you. I promise."

He believed her.

Samantha and Richard never met outside the office. They were both workaholics and nobody suspected anything from their late hours. It was no secret that Richard had only gone home early after Adam was born. Now he was simply back to normal.

Days passed fast between their busy schedules and their anxiety around spending time together after everyone had left. Today, after Constance's visit, Richard and Sam had to endure an eternity of dealing with patients, and at the end of the day, a meeting with the surgeons. Sitting on opposite ends of the large conference table, the two only glanced at each other once.

The first topic was Constance and the breast surgery she was now determined to have. She had already talked to Moore, and he wanted Richard's suggestions.

Richard was in no mood. "Let's make a separate meeting for that tomorrow. What are our other topics?"

They discussed a few other patients and Tyler said,

"I think we should hire Peter Brown. I had a chance to talk to him during the memorial, and he's good. We can use another anesthesiologist."

"I agree," said Sullivan. "Things are getting busier with three facial surgeons, Richard. We need him now."

"Are we voting?" said Stein with a playful expression. "If Jones recommends him, it's fine with me."

"I know I'm his friend and it may sound biased," said Jones, "but he went to Harvard like most of you and is working at a great hospital. How bad can he be?"

Richard was quiet, his mind more on how to juggle Constance and Samantha for a year than on who would be their next *gas passer*—a derogatory nickname for anesthesiologists he'd never use out loud. "All right guys. I told Jones we weren't ready for it, but I guess now we are. If there isn't anything else, I'll just ask Samantha to stay so we can discuss the details of Brown's offer."

It was already 5:45 p.m. and everyone was eager to leave.

When they were alone, Samantha moved to a chair beside Richard. "I'm not here to give you a hard time. I'm just confused. One minute you hate the woman, the other you're laughing and kissing. What did I miss?"

"I'm afraid I can't tell you."

Samantha expected any answers except that one. They were already talking low and her voice came out as a whisper. "What?"

"Sam, I care a lot about you and—"

"You *care a lot* about me?"

Richard smiled. He'd never meant the L word when using it. It was almost painful to pronounce it. "I love you, and I don't wanna lie to you."

"So don't. I'll support you, whatever it is."

He looked at Sam, her expression so sincere he wished he were a bit more trusting. "All I can say is that Constance knows about a big mistake of my past. If I leave her, she'll ruin me."

Sam chuckled sadly. "That sounds like a line a married man would tell his mistress. I hope you know I don't need excuses if you decide to go back to your wife."

There was staff still working on that floor, and it wouldn't be prudent for Richard to move closer to comfort Samantha. He grabbed her hand under the table. "I wanna be with you. It's just better not to bring you into this. Please trust me."

She looked into his eyes. "I do, and I always noticed you seemed uncomfortable around her. Now I know why, and regardless of us, I wouldn't like you to have to keep pretending."

"I won't and here's the plan." While Richard wouldn't reveal his involvement in Sally Landry's murder, he shared Constance's new proposal.

"A year?" Sam shook her head. "I understand it's a shit load of money, but—"

"Two hundred million and she promised to give me half."

"Yeah, but she said if you left now, she wouldn't tell your secret and you could have the clinic. Are you sure you wanna wait?"

"It's not just the money. I don't trust her. If she talks, the best-case scenario is that my career's over."

Samantha looked at her hands, then back at Richard. "Seems like a very juicy secret, and I'm worried. If you want my support, you need to tell me at least this. Did you kill someone?"

"No." He truly believed he hadn't. What happened to Sally had been an accident.

"I meant malpractice," Sam clarified. "Something you may have needed the Carlton's money and influence for to make go away."

"No. But if I leave after her generous peace offer, Constance may use what happened to destroy me."

"And if you wait?"

"If I pretend to give her a second chance and in one year ask for a divorce, there's a bigger chance things will be fine."

"Or, because she's nuts, she's gonna get angry and screw you anyways."

"You're right, but hear me out." Richard told Sam he had no personal assets or savings because until this new deal, his income was going straight to the family fund as payback. He did not mention the blackmail, making it sound like it was payback for the clinic, not his cheating, and concluded with, "It's possible that in a year's time Constance'll trick me, but if this goes wrong then, I'll at least have enough money to defend myself."

"I see." Sam needed no more details. Richard couldn't win any fights against the Carltons being broke.

He tried to reassure her with his eyes. "I know I'm asking you too much, but I think it'll be worth it. Can you stand by me?"

Sam was silent for a while, then nodded slowly, as if fighting the logic of what she was agreeing with. She glanced at the door, which at that hour was unlocked. "I wish you could hold me."

That day Brain had thought about the love birds as well. Love was so cute. So dumb. No matter how intelligent, everyone made mistakes when they were in love. Richard would be no different.

Samantha left Richard's office and stayed another hour in her own. Later Richard went to see her. He spent only ten minutes there. Maybe a kiss, a hug. Too short even for a quickie, but they didn't seem to be able to stay away from each other.

*How wonderful!* That gave Brain a marvelous idea.

# 28

CONSTANCE NORMALLY DIDN'T sleep well the night prior to her plastic surgeries. She and Richard had put their house up for sale and were staying in the family's penthouse at the Four Leaf Towers until they decided where to go next.

This time Constance was more restless than usual, and the cold only served to heighten her foreboding. She reached over to wake up Richard.

"What's wrong?" He was half asleep, lingering in a dream that didn't involve Constance.

"I'm scared."

He rubbed his eyes. "If you don't feel good about the surgery, we can cancel it."

"No. I just want you to hold me like you did before my surgeries in Brazil."

Richard did and, her head on his chest, Constance

said, "Those days were wonderful, weren't they? Maybe our new home should be there."

Peter wore a multicolored surgical hat and Constance recognized him right away. "I'm so glad you're working for us now! You were a doll during my delivery."

"You were a wonderful patient. We'll have a one-on-one before the surgery, but I see everything seems fine on your chart. No health issues. No allergies."

"Yes, honey. I've probably had plastic surgery more times than you've put people under."

They laughed and Peter said, "See you soon!"

After so many surgeries, Constance was comfortable in the clinic. The third floor, where the surgical center was located, was a playground from which she always returned looking prettier.

Alone in the pre-op room, Constance dueled over the fact that Richard had advised against that procedure before and now was rolling with it. Did it mean he no longer cared? And what if something went wrong? So much surgery had been done in that area.

The problem was that she had worked hard to achieve perfection, then pregnancy destroyed everything. She couldn't fix the rest of her body and let her breasts look like that.

She examined her naked torso in the mirror and saw her firm, gorgeous breasts hanging. No other human eye would see what she did. To her, they looked wasted, saggy. An old woman's breasts.

*I'm being a child,* she decided. She had the best plastic

team in the country and Richard knew Pitanguy's every move. He'd gone through the entire plan with Moore and there would be no issues. She wouldn't let the ugly girl inside her scare her out of what she needed to do.

Constance put on the lilac medical gown she'd had designed exclusively for the clinic and waited, only wishing she could take a Valium. Maybe two.

Since Constance would be already under anesthesia for the breast surgery, she asked Tyler and Jones to do *a little something* here and there. The two facial surgeons, then Moore and Brown, would come to see her individually in the pre-op room. That was common practice in the institute. It relaxed the patients and made them feel safe with the entire team.

Brain arranged to be the last one. "How are you doing, Mrs. Wilken?"

Constance laughed at his feigned formality. "Very well, Doctor." A second later, she shook her head. "Liar. I'm terrified."

"Please don't be. We'll take wonderful care of you."

"I know. Breasts are my soft spot."

"I know. Maybe we can do something to relax you." He got a small bottle out of his white coat. "This is a light sedative that won't affect the procedure. I have one myself whenever I'm tense. Just don't drink too much water."

"You're an angel. Richard is so anal. I begged him for a Valium, and he said absolutely no drugs before the surgery."

"He meant nothing strong. But if he said so, please don't say I gave you anything or you'll get me in trouble."

"I won't."

He waited until Constance took the pill. They shared a smile of complicity, and he tapped the intercom. "She's ready."

Constance entered the operating room at 8:10 a.m. Moore positioned himself to her right, with Richard beside him. Tyler and Jones stood at her left. Constance was so used to the process, she enjoyed being awake as the doctors drew the markups for the operation. She felt confident when Moore finished his lines across her breasts, and Richard said, "It'll be perfect."

Tyler smiled at Constance. "My turn."

In five minutes, Tyler's markup was done, and Jones followed.

Peter assumed his position at Constance's head. "Okay, pretty lady. I heard you love Brazil, so, ready for a caipirinha?

Constance's smile relaxed when Peter finished administering the general anesthesia.

Moore took over and was doing his second incision when the alarms in the room started to go off. "What's wrong?"

Peter was in his seat monitoring Constance's vitals. "God, she's in arrhythmia!"

"What the fuck!" screamed Richard. "Why?"

"I don't know! Her vitals are crashing!" Peter said.

Code blue was called, and the room exploded in activity.

"Clear!" Richard yelled as he placed the paddles to Constance's chest.

The incisions in her breast didn't help. A nurse tried to contain the bleeding whenever she wasn't forced to pull away from the patient as electric current was delivered to her heart.

Three attempts. Flatline.

"Let me try, Richard," said Tyler.

"No! She's my wife."

"My point exactly." And by Tyler's look, Richard understood he meant that legally it would be better if he didn't get involved. He stepped aside.

"Clear!" Tyler called out.

"She's still flatlining!" said Peter. "Adrenaline?"

"Try it!" said Moore. "Quickly!"

Their resuscitation efforts lasted almost twenty minutes. Constance was pronounced dead at 9:03 a.m.

# 29

VICTORIA'S PAIN EXPLODED in the form of fury. She demanded Peter Brown to be fired immediately and sued him for malpractice. The police collected testimonials from the medical team and after the autopsy concluded that Constance's cause of death was massive heart and respiratory failures due to incompatibility between recently taken psychiatric drugs and general anesthesia.

No one could believe that Constance had died, and so shortly after Adam. And yet, the fact that she did, combined with her mental health history, also brought back speculations about a suicide attempt. Several gossip magazines had headlines like, "Did Connie Wilken plan to die on the operating table?"

To add to her parents' misery, instead of a traditional burial, Constance would be cremated. What a circus the media would have had if they'd gotten their hands on the note Constance had entrusted her lawyer along with her funeral instructions.

*After all I've done for my body, I refuse to leave it to the worms.*

*May my ashes travel in the wind, mix with the waves, and feed the earth. This way, I'll be beautiful forever.*

There was a memorial service at Saint Martin's, and despite the massive size of the church, seats did not seem to suffice for so many mourners. It wasn't that Constance was loved. With her eccentricities, philanthropy, and beauty obsession, she had become a celebrity in her own way. The place was flooded with curious eyes willing to collect a final moment with the heir of an empire marked by tragedy since childhood.

With its dark wood panels and green wallpaper, Walter Lehman's office belonged more in Victorian London than in Houston. It had a foreboding atmosphere. A place where people planned and protected their assets or sat anxiously or sad to listen from the dead.

Lehman seemed even older and smaller behind his enormous desk. Timothy and Victoria sat on a two-seat couch to Lehman's right, and Richard in an armchair to the left.

"Ladies and gentlemen, I'm sorry for your loss. This is Mrs. Constance Carlton Wilken's will in effect to be probated. Before I read it, be advised that I requested a copy of Mrs. Wilken's autopsy, because her will has a clause regarding the circumstances of her death."

"What circumstances?" Victoria asked, suddenly alarmed.

"Whether or not it was a natural death."

"For Christ's sake," said Timothy. "What difference does it make?"

*Why can't people wait until I'm done?* Lehman contained his irritation. "It would affect how much money Dr. Wilken would inherit."

Victoria's eyes darted at Richard. "So, she thought you might kill her."

"What are you talking about?" Richard said, hoping stupid Constance hadn't spoken to Victoria about Sally.

"My daughter was clever about money, Richard, and she never trusted that you would stay long. Now I see that she also suspected you might try to get rid of her!"

Timothy turned to Lehman. "Would you give us a moment, please?"

"Of course."

"Hold your horses, Victoria. It's Richard you're talking about. He's always been wonderful to our daughter, and we know she wasn't easy."

"Oh, yeah? Then why would she do that?"

"I don't know, but it wouldn't be the first strange thing she did; and the police said there was nothing suspicious about her death. Either Brown made a mistake, or Connie secretly popped some pills. In any case, her death had nothing to do with Richard."

"Did you know he cheated on Connie when they were engaged? What if he were doing the same now and wanted his rich wife out of the way?"

"Victoria, that's out of line," Timothy said.

"Not for me! You should have seen his face when Connie returned home. He was full of hatred. Then suddenly, he's a sweet husband again, and she dies? Something's wrong. I don't care what the police said!"

"I've had enough!" said Richard. "I know what it's like losing a child, Victoria. I just lost mine. But I won't sit here and listen to your wild accusations. I think we should chill and hear what Lehman has to say."

After a moment, Victoria nodded at Timothy. "Go get him."

Lehman returned and continued as robotically as he had begun. "Mrs. Wilken's death was ruled as unnatural and, being so, these are her wishes."

No one blinked.

"My funds and assets shall be split in two equal parts and distributed between my parents, Victoria and Timothy Carlton, and the Wildlife Conservancy."

Richard was petrified, and Victoria laughed aloud. "I think she really knew you."

"This is absurd!" Richard said. "The police ruled it as an accident, and everyone here knows Constance self-medicated. Even if her death was technically unnatural, this shouldn't affect me!"

Lehman looked up over his reading glasses. "There is more."

"My husband shall receive the amount of ten thousand dollars and have the right of buying out The Wilken Institute of Plastic Surgery owned by me in a period of sixty days."

Victoria laughed even harder, and then her eyes filled with tears. "Oh, Connie. I'm so proud of you, sweetie."

Richard got up. "Lehman, this makes no sense! You know I don't have the money to buy out the institute in sixty days."

"I think that was intentional," Victoria said. "Are we finished here?"

Richard continued reasoning with Lehman. "My point is, you know the terms of my agreements with Constance. The old and the new. I would make more money with her alive than dead. Why would I kill her?"

"Nobody in my office is implying you had anything to do with her death, Dr. Wilken. It's not our place trying to guess why your wife included this clause."

"Fine!" Richard continued. "But I'm not talking about the rest of her money. I'm talking about the clinic! Constance would have given it to me if we'd divorced weeks ago. Can't you at least give me a year to buy it out?"

"That can be arranged if the executor of the will agrees. Mrs. Wilken has appointed her mother."

# 30

AT HOME, VICTORIA didn't seem as triumphant as she'd been in Lehman's office, when Richard had begged—and she'd refused—to extend his time to buy the clinic. She didn't care whether the Institute would continue to be as popular without Richard. She could sell it or let another star surgeon, like Clark Moore or Tyler MacLaine, run it and collect the profits. Her delight would be watching Richard pack his office and leave the place that meant the world to him.

That was a marvelous first step to do justice for her Connie, and yet, far from enough.

Timothy was sitting outside his mansion watching his land, a vast carpet of green grass dotted with centenarian oak trees that disappeared into the horizon.

Timothy loved land, and he owned oodles of the

beautiful land of Texas. Open fields and the land under buildings, houses, schools, and hospitals.

*Who will continue my legacy?* It was a question hammering in Timothy's mind since Victoria could bear no more children. For years, Constance was his Connie who loved riding his horses and following him around as he bought, sold, and built his properties. He'd thought that maybe, even though she was a woman, she could have developed a mind for business. Because she was his only hope, Timothy had been willing to try.

Why had Victoria gotten distracted and let the kid walk away to her fall?

Timothy hadn't lost his Connie now. The strong, curious girl who'd felt like a real Carlton had died after her accident. What came back from the hospital was a Frankenstein monster whose wicked mind caused only trouble and pain. Timothy's hope had been reignited when he saw in Richard everything he admired. Richard was a brilliant doctor and wouldn't personally run the family business. That would be a waste of his talents. But with Richard in the family, Timothy felt he had someone to carry on what he had built. He trusted Richard's entrepreneurial mind and knew he wouldn't let the family's empire be torn apart when he and Victoria died.

Adam's birth had been another miracle. Timothy didn't expect Connie to ever have children, and when that little angel came along, Timothy knew his family name wouldn't follow him to the grave.

Now Constance was gone, Adam was gone, and

Victoria was so enraged she was inventing reasons to blame Richard.

Timothy couldn't allow Richard to be destroyed. That young man was the closest thing to a child he had left. Victoria was still upstairs, and Timothy made a call.

"And there's no way you can dispute the will?" Samantha asked when Richard told her the news.

"I called a lawyer friend and he said it would be a waste of money.

Constance was very well advised. By establishing that her condition for me not to receive her money was simply her *unnatural death*, she left me nothing to argue. I could dispute my involvement in her death, if that was questionable, but not the nature of her death."

"Tricky to the grave."

"Yeah. Apparently the generosity in her recent offers were promises for life, not beyond."

Samantha sat closer and held Richard's hand. "I'm so sorry. You didn't deserve this."

"Well, it's not over yet. Timothy just called me to say he'll lend me the money to buy out the clinic. He'll take care of everything this week."

"That's wonderful! You're lucky he likes you so much."

"I like him too. Constance said her dad always wanted a son, and I filled the gap too well. She was always jealous when he defended me."

"I'll keep my fingers crossed. But I better go. Let's see each other as little as possible these days. We're almost there." Sam headed to door and before leaving, mouthed, "I love you."

"I love you too."

At lunchtime, Victoria was on the phone with her lawyer talking about the malpractice case against Peter Brown. Peter's attorney was building a strong defense based on Constance's mental illness. *The scum*, as Victoria called him, had even unearthed Constance's suicide attempt as a teenager and that after Adam's death, she'd been committed to a psychiatric facility for the same reason.

"There was nothing wrong with the anesthetic," explained her lawyer. "It's the same one your daughter took over a dozen times in that same clinic. Brown has a solid record and there was no evidence that he or anyone else there gave Mrs. Wilken the extra substance found in her bloodstream. We can continue if you like, but I honestly don't think you'll win this case. Against Brown or the clinic."

If evidence didn't point to Peter Brown, Victoria couldn't care less about the case. Suing him was the initial conduit for her pain when she received the news of Constance's death. Now pain turned into strategy. She wanted to dig deeper to see if Richard was involved.

She pondered Richard's affair in those final months in Boston. "Call Dr. Brown, Ryan. I'd like to speak with him."

Peter called Victoria back within the hour. "I was advised not to talk to you, Mrs. Carlton, but curiosity got the best of me. What can I do for you?"

"I'm considering dropping the case, Dr. Brown. Would you meet me to discuss the terms?"

"Why don't we let our lawyers do that?"

"I don't mean legal terms. I want to ask you a favor."

Peter met Victoria at the lounge of the Four Seasons that afternoon.

"Thank you for coming, Doctor." After a handshake, Victoria went straight to the point. "I suspect my son-in-law may be responsible for my daughter's death."

"That's a big accusation. He was cleared by the police."

"Do you think it's possible?"

"I really don't think so. Richard seemed to be pretty in love with your daughter."

"Well, let me be the judge of that. If you can throw light on a few issues, I'll drop the case and send a press release to the media to clear your name."

"Well that would be great. What do you want to know?"

"I heard that you and Richard were contemporaries at Harvard."

"Correct."

"My daughter told me he'd had an affair with one of his colleagues right before they got married. Do you know who she was?"

Peter could still see Richard entering the residents' locker the morning after Sally Landry's murder. When Peter delivered the news, Richard's reaction had been so cold he remembered thinking, *How can I love this man? If he doesn't care that his lover was murdered, he's truly heartless.*

Now Peter wondered if Richard had been pretending to be cold to camouflage an affair with a married woman, or because he'd had something to do with Sally's death.

"You thought of something," Victoria said. "I can see it in your face."

"Nothing important."

"Dr. Brown, my daughter believed that Richard had a strong connection with this woman. It wasn't that long ago, and they may still be together. If you and several of your colleagues moved here, she may also be around. If you suspect someone, please tell me her name."

Peter considered his answer. While he wanted to hurt Richard, this would be throwing him in the fire. A woman like Victoria Carlton would hire someone to dig deep, and she could find more than an affair. The idea of hurting Richard still hurt Peter, the usual illogical mechanism that had kept him so long in his obsession. He considered saying a random name that would take Victoria nowhere. But why protect Richard this time, if he had fired him and not given a shit if he took the blame for Constance's death? Fuck Richard. He couldn't help loving him. He owed him no loyalty.

"You don't need to worry about that woman, Mrs. Carlton. She was murdered a few months before Richard moved here."

# 31

Victoria rushed home and relayed to Timothy what Peter Brown had told her. How Sally Landry died, why her husband had been exempted as a suspect, and why the police closed the case as a robbery gone wrong.

Timothy remained silent and Victoria said, "Did you hear what I said?"

"Yes."

"How can you be so calm? Dr. Brown said the murder happened right before Richard moved here, which matches the time Connie said he was having the affair. If he killed this woman, he may have killed Connie!"

"Victoria, having a fling before the wedding doesn't even make Richard a philanderer, much less a murderer."

"Are you going to side with him on this one too?"

In forty-two years of marriage, it was the first time Victoria had raised her voice during an argument.

"Darling, I think your grieving is making you paranoid. If there was something wrong either in Connie's or this lady's death, the police would have found out. Besides, our Connie could be eccentric, but she wouldn't have married Richard if she thought he could be a murderer."

"I'm not paranoid. I'm flabbergasted that our daughter dies, and you have no desire to discover what happened to her!"

It was Timothy's turn to raise his voice. "I know what happened to Connie!

She played with fire having all those unnecessary surgeries and taking too many drugs all these years. Nobody killed her, Victoria! Her body had just had enough!"

"All right. If you won't help me investigate Richard's possible involvement in Connie's death, I'll go to Boston and tell the police that he was fucking this Sally Landry. Maybe they didn't know about it, and he can get what he deserves."

"No you won't! We've had enough crap involving our family without you accusing Richard of murder!"

"Richard's no longer family."

"He is to me, and I'm loaning him the money to buy the clinic and get back on his feet."

"Over my dead body you will!"

Timothy's face was so red Victoria thought he'd

have a heart attack. He closed his eyes and rubbed his forehead.

He was mute for a long while and Victoria asked, "Are you okay, Tim?"

Timothy drew a deep breath. "Nothing will bring our Connie back." He spoke as if uttering each word was a painful effort. "We always disagreed about everything involving her, but this time, we need to be on the same page, Vic. No matter how terrible we feel."

Victoria came to sit beside Timothy. She put a hand on his shoulder and rested her head against it. "You're right. Nothing will bring her back."

"And going to the police will hurt us too," he said. "Do you want to tarnish our good name, our business, only to harm Richard?"

*You bet,* Victoria thought, and she would if needed. For the moment, though, Timothy's help was more urgent. "Okay, honey. But I can't just let this go. I won't talk to the police if you don't loan any money to Richard."

After a long pause, Timothy said, "You have my word." In slow motion, he got up. "I need something to eat."

"Good idea. I'll join you soon."

When Timothy had disappeared down the hallway, Victoria called her lawyer. "Ryan, I need a private investigator in Boston."

# 32

TIMOTHY WAS AT Richard's door the following morning. "Is it too early for a scotch?"

It was 10:15, but Richard said, "Not at all."

While Richard was at the bar fixing their drinks, Timothy advanced toward the familiar living room and sat at his favorite chair by the window. "I have bad news. I won't be able to loan you the money."

"I figured when you said you needed to see me in person." He handed Timothy a glass. "Victoria must have given you a hard time."

"Yes, and the reason I didn't fight back was that something more serious came up, and I wanted to warn you." Timothy shared what Peter Brown had told Victoria about Sally Landry's murder. "I couldn't risk this coming out. Victoria is angry and not herself since Connie died. She could make a mess."

Richard couldn't believe that Constance had died without saying a word about Sally, and now a near stranger had served him on a plate to his hateful mother-in-law. His temples were throbbing with tension, and it took him a while to recover from the blow. At last, he said, "You're right, Tim, and thank you for being so gracious about it. You didn't even ask me what happened."

"It's none of my business. I had my own indiscretions when I was young, and I'm not here to judge you."

"I'm more impressed you didn't ask me about the murder."

Tim emptied his glass and Richard refilled it. "So much shit happens without our planning it. When I was twenty-two, I killed a man by accident in Key Biscayne. He was drunk and entered my boat while I was docked in the marina late at night. I was stronger and dragged him out of and pushed him toward the platform. He took three steps, lost his balance, and fell in the water. My first instinct was to throw a rope to him, but the bastard started screaming that I'd attacked him, and I stopped. When he went under again, I let him. He was a local bum and the police assumed he'd drowned. After that, I never read any situation just in black and white."

Richard owed Timothy a story, but not even his pillow would hear the truth. "I see," he said. "And I'll reciprocate your trust." He relayed his sexual escapades with Sally and being at her place before she was murdered, omitting the strangling accident and tampering with the scene. "As you can imagine, if I'd told the police about the affair, Sally's husband, who was a decent fellow, would have endured an extra layer of pain, and I would have become a suspect for no reason. So I stayed quiet."

"You did the right thing, and we should keep this under wraps forever."

"How do you know Victoria won't tell?"

"She's a good woman. It's her maternal instincts going awry now. If it seems that you were punished enough by losing your money and the clinic, with time, she'll let it go. I'm just sorry the price is so high for you."

"I know. Thank you for trying to help."

"I always will if I can."

Brain found the sealed envelope under his front door. No stamps. Delivered in person. The note started with, "I hope you don't mind—I got your address at the clinic."

He read the rest of the message, and even though there was no signature, he recognized the logo in the upper-right corner of the stationery. Two very particular white lilies with golden stems. They were also present in a familiar business card Brain had received. He remembered complimenting the card owner on the elegant design.

Victoria Carlton's reputation of being an unstoppable train when she put an idea in her mind preceded her. Whenever she appeared in the media, it was never like an old socialite showing off a new gown or flashy jewelry. Victoria defended important causes and was diplomatic and persuasive enough to be influential. She knew how to leverage her money and command power through her family name. Not someone he would like as an enemy.

With a mix of concern and curiosity, Brain reread the note.

I know about Sally Landry.

Reflection Pool at Hermann Park.

3 pm.

Brain was already there when Victoria arrived. She looked at him, alone on a bench reading the paper, seeming not to have a care in the world. How deceiving looks could be.

There were dozens of passersby, men walking dogs, women pushing baby carriages. Victoria felt safe confronting him there. He too seemed to hate Richard and want his revenge plan to stay a secret. They would be stronger together.

Victoria sat beside Brain and told him how she'd learned about Sally Landry. "My investigator in Boston found nothing connecting her to Richard. But he investigated Sally's inner circle, and that got me to you. It didn't take me much to realize why you came to work with Richard. He killed Sally, right?"

Brain nodded.

"Why'd you let him get away?"

After a while, with his eyes on the reflective water, he said, "Because jail wasn't enough, and back then, I could have incriminated myself if I'd done something against him. I knew he would move here and start a practice, so I waited for him to build up his life and think he's safe. Now whatever happens will have no connection to that case."

"I'm impressed. I wish I had your patience."

"Patience, Mrs. Carlton, is like finding a rough diamond and polishing it until it sparkles."

"Do you think he killed my daughter?"

"Yes."

Victoria sighed. "I wouldn't be able to stand beside him and be friendly. You are a cold man."

"When I have to be."

"And what was your plan when you came to Houston?"

"I wanted to gain his trust so I could find the best way to hurt him."

"And did you find it?"

"Just did."

"Can some financial encouragement make your diamond sparkle faster?"

"Money always helps, but if you know I'll take care of Richard, why get your hands dirty?"

"Because whatever you're planning for him will also do justice for my daughter. I want to reward you."

"And your husband?"

"He won't know."

# 33

MOORE HAD NO surgeries that day and had been with a real estate broker all morning looking for his new acquisition. Money had the fantastic power of changing realities overnight. For good and for bad.

It had been worth waiting, and soon he'd be able to remove his mask. The small fortune he'd received would put him on top of his game when Richard fell. It would be such a delight to watch!

Richard went to Samantha's home for the first time. She opened the door with concern on her face. "This is no good, is it?"

Richard told her about Timothy and that none of the banks he had visited would give him the amount he needed without assets or grantors.

Samantha couldn't stop shaking her head. "It's so

unfair. I can't believe they'd take away everything you built."

"I'm upset of course, but the worst thing was losing my son. The clinic and the money I can remake."

Samantha squeezed his hand. "Of course you can!"

"And honestly, I'm so relieved she's gone."

"Me too." Sam managed a smile. "And if you're completely broke, I know a place you can crash."

At the Institute, Richard met with the surgeons first, told them the news about not being able to buy out the clinic and that he was leaving. After their initial shock, Sullivan asked him, "What are you going to do?"

"Not sure yet."

Jones was perplexed. "I'm so sorry, Richard. After all you've done here, I can't picture you out there looking for a job."

"But he won't have trouble getting one," said Stein, trying to lighten the mood.

Richard couldn't smile and Sullivan said, "That'll depend on what the Carltons broadcast about Richard's leaving here, right?"

Richard nodded. "I'll cross that bridge when I get there. Regarding my successor, Victoria Carlton wants Tyler to be in charge."

With all eyes on him, Tyler said, "Me?"

"Yeah, she said you're competent as a doctor and have leadership traits she admires."

"Jeez, I'm grateful but uncomfortable. I haven't been here long."

"Long enough to make a great impression," said Stein, clearly upset. And Richard intervened, "Before this goes the wrong way, let me say this. The Carltons like Tyler as a friend, but it doesn't mean their assessment is wrong. Even though I had no voice on that decision, it's not a bad one."

"Should I talk to her?" said Tyler.

"No. What I would recommend, if you guys still respect me, is that you work as a team as we always did. Victoria is trying to punish me, and she doesn't give a shit what happens to this clinic. If you love your jobs, there's no time for resentment; cooperate with Tyler and help each other make this work."

Everyone nodded, some more enthusiastically than others, and they moved on to figuring out a plan to continue to serve Richard's patients.

Samantha was at the meeting and faked surprise at every sentence Richard had already told her. It was too soon for them to go public.

Alone with Richard after the meeting concluded, Tyler said, "It doesn't feel right to replace you."

"You've been a great friend, Tyler." Richard looked around. "If I had to lose this, I'm glad it's in your hands. Be smart about it and be careful with Victoria. She kisses you today and poisons your coffee tomorrow."

Tyler smiled. "I will."

Moore had been quiet most of the meeting, reflecting on the past years of his life. He had never liked Richard. *Fake* was the word he used to describe his peer since medical school. But he knew a genius when he saw one, and back in Boston, knowing who Richard was going to marry, Moore couldn't miss the opportunity of starting a high-end practice with him to learn the moves. He decided to implant a smile on his face, play friends, and stay by Richard's side for a few years as the snobbish asshole rose to fame. The experience would brighten Moore's already remarkable resume for when he received his inheritance and could open his own clinic.

Had Richard been the sharing type who proposes a partnership to worthy colleagues, Moore would have warmed toward him. As expected, Richard had remained selfish along the years, and as Moore's uncle's health deteriorated, his fantasies revolved around becoming Richard's meanest competition.

His bachelor uncle had finally died after years battling cancer and left him three million dollars. It had been a long wait, and nothing would have given Moore more pleasure than telling Richard that he was leaving—secretly carrying several of his most lucrative patients.

In every step since he left the conference room after hearing the news of Richard's leaving, Moore thought of the gorgeous building he'd leased thirty-six hours earlier. His plan had played out perfectly, and yet, the news today had overshadowed his happiness.

The day before, he had told Richard that he was leaving and Richard had seemed sorry but absent. Now Moore understood why. If Richard was also leaving the institute, he couldn't care less that Moore was opening his own practice. The fun of Moore's vendetta had been robbed from him.

He stopped outside his office door and read his name on the golden plate. He'd been just another doctor in Richard Wilken's kingdom. A plate soon to be replaced.

Moore laughed, angry at himself for having just committed his money to another clinic when he could have bought this one. He could even picture Richard leaving the building as workers changed the sign outside to "The Moore Institute of Plastic Surgery." *That* would have been painful to Richard. But again, the bastard was ahead of him.

Moore entered his office and ignoring the passersby, slammed the door.

At the end of the day, the rest of the staff, along with the surgeons, who already knew, gathered at the clinic's plaza and Richard spoke. "After the events of the past few months, you can imagine that my family, or what's left of it, is not in a good place. I'd like to tell you that I'll be leaving effective immediately."

There were gasps and murmurs and Richard said, "This won't affect your jobs." Everyone went silent and he proceeded. "My in-laws inherited the clinic, and after the accident with my wife, they don't think I'm the best doctor to continue to run this place."

Most employees frowned and shook their heads in disapproval.

Richard smiled. "It was an honor to work with

each and every one of you, and I wish you all the best of success. Dr. MacLaine will take over, so you're in great hands."

Handshakes followed, and some of the nurses and secretaries crossed the line and hugged Richard, saying he would be missed.

Samantha watched. One part of her was devastated that Richard was losing his dream; another was elated that they could finally be together.

Moving in with Samantha Reeves was the first impulse Richard gave in to. While the ten thousand dollars he had received from Constance's estate wasn't a fraction of what he needed to keep up his lifestyle, it didn't mean he had to succumb to pressure or accept charity. Sam had invited him to give it a shot, and it felt right. She was so easygoing, so understanding, and if there were any questions that she might have been seeing him for his money, that option was off the plate. Samantha didn't blink an eye when Richard lost his fortune. Her feelings seemed real; and, another novelty for Richard, so were his.

Samantha lived in the suburb of Bellaire in a home she'd bought a few years earlier when she left her job in Dallas. The main floor consisted of a living area, a dining room connected to a kitchen, a bathroom, and a laundry room. Upstairs, there were two bedrooms, two bathrooms, and a porch. Most of Richard's personal items, including the art he had received as gifts, were allowed to be removed from his previous home.

Samantha had given him the grand tour in a previous visit, and Richard knew his belongings alone would fill up her entire dining room, so he put everything in storage and brought only the essentials that fit in a pair of suitcases.

"Are you sure you're not just spending the weekend?" Sam joked.

"I don't need much to be happy."

"I could see that in the years I worked for you. A real frugal existence."

Richard loved the sound of Sam's laughter. It was a plausible force that carried warmth and lightness, and he couldn't get enough of it.

"Seriously," she said. "I know it's gonna be tough for you to adjust to a normal life, but you told me you weren't born rich, and I hope with enough love and good will, you'll be happy here."

The place was modest, and yet, as he looked around, Richard could tell that every piece of furniture, every planted pot, and every painting on the wall had been carefully chosen to create a welcoming atmosphere. "I'm sure I will."

Sam guided him to the guest bedroom. "This was my home office. I moved my desk downstairs so you can have this room."

"You brought me all the way here to tell me we'll sleep in separate bedrooms?"

Sam's smile wouldn't leave her face. "Who said anything about sleeping here?" She kissed him. "The master bedroom will be ours as a couple, but you were used to tons of space. Having a room only for your stuff may help a bit with your transition."

"That's very thoughtful. Thank you."

It was early Saturday afternoon, and Sam headed downstairs to fix them lunch while Richard unpacked. He finished quickly and stood at the top of the staircase, as he did at his mansion in River Oaks. How many times he had awoken in the middle of the night and stood at the gigantic staircase appraising the expensive furniture and art below. He was so proud to own them. Richard had enjoyed stopping before a particular large painting in a silver frame. How powerful he'd felt being the highest bidder for the Picasso.

Richard's mind traveled back to the Fifth Avenue apartment he'd visited as a child. His excursions through Manhattan as a young man learning about the world of the rich. He had worked so hard, had been so determined. How had a mistake that lasted the length an orgasm put him in this position? He cursed the day he got involved with Sally Landry, and even more, the one he met Constance Carlton.

Still, despite it all, he had become the celebrity doctor he'd dreamed of becoming. Had married into money and made his own. The greatest treasure, however, had been becoming a father and discovering that through Adam, he could have lived forever.

*What does life reserve for me now?*

"Traumatized or daydreaming?" Sam asked from the lower level. The table was ready, and she was filling it with food.

Following the delicious aroma, Richard came downstairs. "Neither. Exploring."

Sam set a tray on the table and turned back to Richard. "I won't pretend to know how you're feeling. I can only say I'll be here to help you get everything back."

He came closer, eyes on hers. "You've been wonderful to me."

"And I know nothing will ever replace Adam, but if one day you're ready, I'd love to have a child with you."

Richard found himself smiling. He wasn't sure that child would ever exist. What mattered was how close he felt to Sam at the moment. He hugged her, and her hair smelled like home. A scent long gone in his childhood memories.

Richard closed his eyes. After a lifetime of chasing wealth, he had discovered what being rich truly meant.

Brain would have made a fine detective. Once without the means to pay for one, he had to do his own investigations and had acquired several important skills. Following people and picking locks were his specialties.

When asked by his colleagues, Richard was very mysterious about his new address. He'd say he was at hotels, maybe out of town with friends. Only Brain knew of his affair with Samantha Reeves and that the love birds would probably move in together. Brain followed Richard a few times to make sure, including the day Richard went to storage and when he arrived at Samantha's with his luggage. It was perfect that they'd share the same roof, for whatever tragedy was about to happen to Richard would happen in that house.

Brain knew Samantha's and Richard's schedules that afternoon and confidently walked into their yard and toward the back door, which he easily picked.

Inside, the air was cool and pleasant, and he had a solid hour to study the place for his plan. It was a cozy middle-class home and Brain smiled. A greedy motherfucker like Richard must be insanely in love to go live there instead of renting his own apartment with the money he'd received.

Love could be a powerful healing or destructive force, and Brain was enjoying working with that new scenario. Love had even helped him find the perfect scapegoat. An idiot whose dark thoughts were chronicled in a journal locked in the third drawer of his desk.

The police would love that.

# 34

ALONG THE YEARS, Richard and Timothy developed the habit of meeting for breakfast every other Thursday to catch up about their businesses. Since Richard was no longer welcome anywhere near Victoria, he couldn't go to their house as usual, and Timothy met him at a café.

"I'm living with Samantha Reeves," Richard said. "We've been discreet to honor Constance's memory, but I wanted you to know it from me."

Timothy took a sip of his cappuccino. "I suspected you two were involved."

Richard was puzzled. "How?"

"Adam's memorial. She looked at you like she was suffering your pain. I remember hoping you stayed with Connie but also hoping you found solace wherever you could."

"Thank you for not sharing this with Victoria. She already thought of me as a murderer."

"I wouldn't. Women make these things far bigger than they are."

Richard's hand tingled as he stirred his coffee, and he massaged it. It was the second time that day.

"Are you okay?" Timothy asked. "You're a bit pale."

"Too much stress. My blood pressure's been all over the place."

Timothy laughed. "I'd say go check it out, but you doctors never walk your talk."

"You're right."

"You were telling me about Samantha Reeves. Are you happy?"

"Yeah. I never thought I could forgive Constance for risking Adam's life, and I was in such grief. Samantha brought me back on my feet."

"Sometimes having an affair is the only way to make a marriage last, and Victoria wasn't half as hard as Connie was." Timothy's eyes brimmed with tears. "I loved my daughter, but God forgive me, I'd never marry a woman like her. So you have my blessings."

"Thank you, Tim. I hope I'll continue to deserve your affection."

"Same here."

The two finished their coffee talking about topics they both enjoyed. Before getting into his car, Timothy hugged Richard. "Good luck, son!"

When the taxi dropped him home, Richard found it strange that Samantha's car was still there. It was almost noon, and she should be in the clinic. He unlocked the front door and found the house torn apart. Reading lamps smashed, planters broken, the contents of shelves and drawers on the floor.

*Sam!* Richard rushed upstairs to find the same signs of destruction along the hallway. He went straight to the main bedroom, and there she was, lying naked on the bed, her lifeless eyes staring at him.

"No, no, no!" Richard jumped on the bed and, despite the clear signs Samantha was dead, checked her pulse. It wasn't until he saw the strangle marks on her neck that he had a feeling of déjà vu. He paid attention to the details around him and noticed that the paintings had been removed from the walls, the vanity table's drawers were open, and the contents of the closet were scattered on the floor.

Richard sobbed and looked back at Samantha. He saw the cuts and purple marks on her arms and hips. The blood between her legs. The scene was a replica of what he had created in Sally's bedroom.

Richard remembered the anonymous caller and knew immediately that Constance had lied. It had never been she who'd called John Landry. Someone else knew about the affair and knew he had killed Sally.

Unlike the last time he'd been in a crime scene, Richard disregarded the forensic details he'd been so particular about. He didn't care if he might be incriminating himself. He held Sam in his arms and cried, kissing the top of her head. "I'm sorry. I'm so sorry."

Dizzy, like he'd thrown back a bottle of whiskey, Richard came down the steps clinging to the bannister. He couldn't believe some revengeful monster had done this to Sam to punish him. His copycat had even taken Sam's mother's ring, which never left her finger, and broke the back door's lock, just like Richard had done at Sally's. A robbery gone wrong.

The sickest touch was the cactus pots on the dining room floor. Sam didn't like cactus—Sally did. Whoever did it knew Sally very well. The bastard had actually brought those cacti, so Richard knew it was payback.

It could only be John Landry, and Richard had become so famous anyone could easily find him. Pain turned into rage. Richard called the Massachusetts General Hospital in Boston to learn of John Landry's whereabouts.

"Dr. Landry works evenings," the operator said. "Would you like to leave a message, Dr. Wilken?"

Landry still lived in Boston, but if he'd taken yesterday off, he could have had time for the flights back and forth. "This is an emergency, and I can't locate him at home. Was he working last night?"

While the operator checked Landry's schedule, Richard's entire left arm tingled, and his head felt like a ticking bomb. His blood pressure must be through the roof.

"Yes, Dr. Wilken," the operator finally said. "He left the hospital at seven this morning."

Landry was in Boston. It wasn't him.

Richard hung up, too overwhelmed to decide what to do next. What he knew was that he had nothing left to lose. He would tell the police what he had done in Boston, and whoever had done this to Sam would pay for it, even if he had to go to jail with him.

As Richard started calling the police, he remembered Sally telling him about her family. A brother who adored her and was also a doctor.

"He's complicated," Sally said. "Brilliant, but very angry. I'm the only one who keeps him under control."

Richard stopped. What the hell was Sally's maiden name?

The memory came to him accompanied by a debilitating headache. His temples throbbing, Richard let go of the phone. His vision was blurry, and the house spun so fast he could no longer stand.

He collapsed murmuring a familiar name.

# 35

As PETER PARKED in front of Samantha's house, he saw the door open. *Good.* That would save him the nervousness of ringing the bell and waiting for Richard. He had probably seen his car approach and was already coming out. He still didn't know what was so urgent. Another inquiry about Constance's surgery? A favor to ask? An apology? Whatever it was, he was glad Richard had sent him that message.

No one came out of the house, and Peter started walking toward the front door. As he came closer, he realized something was very wrong. The living area looked like a war zone, and in a corner, near the couch, Richard lay on the floor.

Peter ignored the possibility that a criminal might still be there. All he saw was Richard. Peter rushed to him and kneeled down. Richard's eyes were open, and his head moved side to side. He seemed disoriented. There was no blood or visible wounds, and Peter assumed it was a concussion. He examined Richard's head, and there was no indication that anybody had hit him. Richard grabbed Peter's arm weakly and said, "Sam..." He tried to elaborate but could form no more words.

"You're having a stroke, Richard. I'll call 911."

Peter never looked for Samantha Reeves. These were precious minutes, and he wanted to enjoy each and every second. He sat on the floor and put Richard's head on his lap. "It'll be better if you stay awake, so I'll try to entertain you."

Peter chuckled at the absurdity that led him to have Richard for a few moments. "You may die, and I certainly will soon, so I want you to know that I always loved you."

Peter caressed Richard's jaw. "I always wanted to do this, and it feels..." He closed his eyes, and when he opened them again, he was crying. "My words escape me too."

Richard's eyes were closing, and Peter said, "Stay with me. They're almost here."

Richard looked up, and yet Peter knew he wouldn't remember anything he said. Holding Richard's hand, he went on talking. "I'm sorry I told Victoria about Sally. She took away your clinic and God knows, maybe even did this." He was crying harder now. "I fucked many things in my life because I was always angry at you. I knew you were straight and would never be mine, but why wasn't I good enough to be your friend?"

Richard closed his eyes and Peter didn't know if he would ever see him again. "I forgive you," he said. "And I love you so, so much."

Peter kissed Richard's lips, then held him in his arms until the paramedics arrived.

# 36

RICHARD AWOKE IN a hospital almost a week later unaware that the only woman he'd ever loved had been buried the day before.

"He's awake!" said a nurse, and a doctor came in to check on him.

"Can you hear me, Richard?"

No response.

The doctor put a light in Richard's face. "Can you follow this?"

Richard's eyes seemed lost, like he'd landed on a different planet.

Timothy had gone to the hospital every day and told the doctors, "Give him the best care money can buy." When he met the neurologist in charge, Timothy asked, "What happened to him?"

"A massive stroke. We weren't sure he would wake.

His body is partially paralyzed. It may or may not come back with rehab."

"And his mind?"

"He understands basic commands, but when I asked if he knew who he was or why he was here, he looked away. Let's give him time."

Timothy patted Richard's arm. "I'll come back tomorrow. Hang in there, son."

The police had eliminated Richard as a suspect when Timothy Carlton testified as his alibi. Two detectives showed up at the hospital when Richard was conscious.

"Do you know who did it, Dr. Wilken?" asked the one in charge.

Richard's mouth wouldn't obey him. His whole body felt foreign. Some parts numb, others heavy as steel. He just stared at the man.

"What about blinking once for *yes* and twice for *no*, Dr. Wilken?"

Richard tried, but he had no control over the muscles of his face. His eyes wouldn't blink on demand. He managed to move two fingers of his right hand, and the younger detective said, "Maybe he can write."

The man held a piece of paper and gave Richard a pen.

He couldn't hold it.

"Please try again, Dr. Wilken. It's important."

Richard couldn't.

As Peter was found in the crime scene after having been fired and sued by Richard's family, he was the prime suspect and had been detained for interrogation and DNA testing. With their communication options exhausted, the main detective asked Richard a direct question: "Was it Peter Brown?"

*No!* Richard wanted to scream, but his frozen neck wouldn't allow him to shake his head. He tried and failed to blink twice as a *no*, and in his frustration, accidentally produced a frown.

The detectives misread his expression and the one in charge said, "I guess that's a *yes*. He seems afraid."

"Yeah he does," said Timothy, who was now standing at the door. "And this kind of pressure can be harmful to his health. He can't help you, detectives. I'd like you to leave."

The police got a warrant to search Peter's apartment, and they found a goldmine. Peter kept a journal chronicling his obsession with Richard, his jealousy, his anger, and his attempts to gain Richard's attention. That evidence discredited Peter's statement that he had been called to Richard's new home to chat, despite the invitation Peter had received. Brain (theoretically Richard) had sent it to Peter, but since it was typed and had no prints, the police assumed Peter typed it himself.

Even though no traces of Peter Brown's DNA were found on Samantha Reeves's body, when the police pieced together that violent crime, Constance's mysterious death, and the fact that both women had been romantically involved with Richard, Peter became the face of a frustrated platonic lover whose obsession had gotten carried away. He was arrested and would face trial. To add to Peter's misfortune, his tests revealed that he was HIV positive, and the information leaked to the media. In those dark days when AIDS was called by conservative groups "the gay plague," and being infected with the virus was often a death sentence, popular opinion was that Peter was a desperate, dying man capable of anything. This time, his lawyer was not optimistic.

Tyler smoothed the large onyx table in Richard's office—now his office—with both hands as if summoning the man's power ingrained in the rock. He smiled, remembering his performance when Richard told him the news in front of the surgical team and he'd pretended to be shocked. Days earlier, Victoria had told him he would replace Richard, and they decided it would be wise for Tyler to appear as if he hadn't been consulted on the matter.

Victoria was really a force of nature and an ally worth having.

Tyler's next appointment knocked at the door, and he asked him to come in.

While Jones had robotically performed three surgeries since the news of Samantha's murder, Richard's stroke, and Peter Brown's arrest, whenever his colleagues talked about these subjects, he unceremoniously left the room.

That morning, Jones had rung Tyler to schedule a tête-à-tête, and Tyler hoped he didn't intend to quit. Morale was understandably low, and Moore had announced he was mercilessly jumping ship in their hardest moment. Tyler couldn't afford losing Jones.

"I'm sorry about Brown," Tyler said after Jones sank into a chair. "After what you told me when we met, I assumed he was more than your friend."

"Thank you," was all Jones managed to say.

"And they're saying he's HIV positive. You should get tested."

"We used protection, but I did. I'm clean."

"Great to hear!"

Jones seemed devastated. His eyes lifeless like someone who'd survived too many tragedies. "I need a break, Tyler. Can you give me a week or two?"

Tyler melted with relief. "Of course, man! I'll postpone the procedures I can't do and cover the rest for you. Come back when you're ready."

Like his colleagues, Brain went to visit Richard a few days after he woke up.

He pulled a chair up to Richard's side. "I saw your charts. Losing Adam, your clinic, then Sam. There's only so much pain a person can take."

Richard's eyes filled with tears.

"I knew you could understand me. It wouldn't be fair if you couldn't. Now that I have your attention." He lowered his voice to a whisper. "I killed Sam... and Constance."

Richard's lips trembled, and Brain wondered if it was from nerves or an attempt to speak. Either was enjoyable to watch. "When you killed my sister and did those atrocities to her body to pretend it was a robbery, I wanted to kill you myself."

As Richard's eyes widened, Brain nodded. "Yep, I'm her brother. I knew you two were together, and in the beginning I rooted for you." There was a moment of silence, as if he was lost in the past, and then Brain said, "Sally played tough. The drinking and drugs were because in the love department, real life never matched her dreams. She told me she wanted you to dump Constance and stay in Boston with her. She was ready to leave Landry, but you wouldn't leave Constance. So I gave you both a push."

A nurse appeared at the door. "Is he okay?"

"Yes, thank you. And don't worry, we work together. I'm Dr. Jones."

# 37

THE NURSE SMILED at Jones. "Nice to meet you, Doctor. His bath will be in an hour."

"I won't be that long."

The woman nodded and closed the door, leaving Richard alone with his enemy.

"As I was saying, *my friend*." Jones squeezed Richard's hand hard enough to hurt him. "I was visiting our mother that week and decided to let my brother-in-law find out about your affair while I was around to support my sister. I wanted Sally to be happy, but she must have spoken up that evening, threatened to tell Constance, and you killed her."

Richard's eyes revealed his desperation and Jones said, "Are you trying to say something?" He grinned. "A bit late for that. You killed the only person who understood me. You're a pig, Richard, and so is Constance. She covered up for your crime."

Jones leaned forward. "You know how many plans I made to destroy your miserable life? I could have denounced you in Boston and you would have rotted in jail. Then I thought, why rush if you were moving to Texas and with a new crime could get the death penalty? I had planned to murder Constance to incriminate you. But your falling for Sam was such a wonderful twist you didn't need to die. At least, not physically."

Jones scanned Richard's immobile body as if assessing the damage on a crashed vehicle. "Shrinks say that after losing someone we consider irreplaceable, if we find an emotional life vest, like you found in Sam, we hold onto it so desperately that if we lose that too, we truly break." His voice triumphant, Jones made a huge effort to keep it down. "I framed Peter so you'd be free to die of pain like I almost did; and if I ever changed my mind, you'd be accessible for me to give you another type of slow death. The stroke worked better than I could've planned."

Jones leaned back in his chair, quiet for a moment, then said, "You are such a poison, Richard, that even to punish you I had to suffer again. I liked Peter, but when you didn't give him that job, he was so mad I suspected there was something between you. That's when I found his journal, and since he was using me, why not use him?" Jones' face suddenly became animated. "But it was so easy with Sam! She let me in, and you should have seen her face when I attacked her." He glanced at the door and contained his laughter. "She was terrified. She fought but had no chance. We surgeons know which buttons to push, don't we?"

Jones placed a hand on Richard's chest and slowly slid it to his throat. "Now we're even, and I hope you'll stay this way forever. Useless. Dueling with your tragic memories and your guilt. Just remember, if you are ever happy, I'll come for you."

With the overwhelming satisfaction of a mission well accomplished, Jones left the hospital with his feet barely touching the ground. He eased his long frame into the seat of his new Mercedes convertible thinking of his new life. New dreams. He had lived for so long in the past; he wanted the word *new* to become his motto. Daydreaming, he turned south onto 1-45, the cool air tossing about his hair. His mind was on what he would do with the money Victoria had paid him. He could start his own practice. He could take a year of sabbatical and travel the world.

The phone brought him back to reality.

"How is he?" It was Victoria.

"As he should be."

"Are you satisfied?"

"Very. Are you?"

She sighed. "I still feel like there's a loose end."

"Your daughter's murderer became a zombie and his accomplice is dead. What could be better?"

"I don't know. You said Richard was the last one to see Connie before the surgery. What if you were busy and missed something? What if someone else helped him?"

"Trust me. I was there and I'm giving you my word."

A pause. "All right. I think a mother always wants more."

"We honored Sally and Connie, Mrs. Carlton. Please find your peace."

Jones arrived home and retrieved his folder from its secret place. That was the next step: to bury the past. He took one last look at each of the clips he'd collected along the years and burned them in the sink. Starting with Sally's murder, the investigations, and the police closing the case. Then, everything about Richard and Constance.

He relived the pain and the hatred. When all the clips turned into ashes, he was empty.

# ONE MONTH LATER

## HOUSTON

A FEW DAYS after awaking from his stroke, Richard had a nervous breakdown and his mind stopped responding to the outside world. He was living at a luxurious hospital. A *recovery resort*, as they sold it, for six figures a year. Timothy paid the bills and was Richard's only visitor. His father-in-law hated to see such a brilliant brain deteriorating. All that energy and charisma going to waste.

While Richard could walk, the stroke rendered his left arm useless, and he never spoke again. He would sometimes seem to have a few moments of clarity when Timothy said something about the past or told a tale about the people they knew; at those times Richard looked at him like he understood. Mostly, he just sat there, his mind in a bubble of his own.

Timothy wasn't even sure Richard recognized him as family. He seemed to enjoy seeing him though, and that was enough. After talking and talking without a word in return, Timothy started bringing a backgammon board. They sat at the tables in the garden where patients played cards and chess or had tea with their guests, shadowed by oak trees surrounding a manmade lake.

As Timothy placed the pieces on the board, he talked. "Last time, I explained the rules. Today, I'll play against myself to show you how it works. Pay close attention." He was excited, as if traveling back in time. "I'm very good at this, Richard, and you will be too. In Monte Carlo, I competed with *la crème de la crème* of Europe!"

Richard's eyes weren't vague that morning. He was focused on each movement, and Timothy smiled. Maybe the game would stimulate Richard's mind and he would leave this place one day.

*A shame Victoria wouldn't join them*, Timothy thought. She would have so many stories to tell Richard about those fun days of Mediterranean summers and backgammon tournaments. Victoria hated Richard. She blamed him for bringing all the misery to their family. All the death. But Timothy couldn't sever the umbilical cord so easily. After a lifetime of dealing with his daughter's mental illness, he could accommodate Richard, with whom he had formed a much stronger bond.

The backgammon board reminded Richard of when he lived in New York. As a teenager, learning the ways of the rich, he was once intrigued by a gorgeous backgammon board in an antique shop.

As he admired the onyx and marble hand-carved pieces, the salesman had told him, "It's backgammon, an old game that's been around for millennia."

"An old game for loaded fellows, right?" Richard had said, full of enthusiasm. "I never heard of it."

The man laughed. "Yes. It appeals to the rich because it's fast and easy to bet. Do you play chess?"

"A bit, with my dad."

"Chess only counts on skills. For backgammon, you play the dice and need luck to be a winner. Skills and luck. Just like in life."

While Richard didn't recall if he'd learned how to play then, he was glad the salesman had been visiting him. He just wished he knew his name.

Richard smiled at the fine gentleman in front of him, then looked back at the board. He would learn now, so when he returned home, he could teach Adam. He hoped Constance wouldn't cause trouble like she did about everything. Thank God they were divorced and he could go live with Sam.

He loved Sam.

## BOSTON

Jones said a silent prayer and placed a bouquet of tulips on Sally's grave. "Justice was done, sister. I won't be returning here."

In the deserted cemetery, an elegant man in a gray suit passed by Jones and murmured, "Good morning."

Jones felt a sudden pain in his chest; then the warm, familiar fluid that stained his hands in every surgery. He turned around and the stranger smiled. Two more silent shots and Jones dove into darkness, his puzzled face kissing the earth.

A light rain was starting to fall and the man in gray opened his umbrella. He kept walking and soon disappeared, leaving Jones's body concealed among the graves.

Across the street, Constance's favorite song was playing. Another private celebration. The forecast had predicted a sunny afternoon and Victoria could already sense the blue skies behind the heavy clouds.

The man in gray exited the cemetery gate and glanced in her direction. A casual nod, and she knew his mission had been accomplished. She started the car and headed to the airport.

Her daughter could rest now.